He had, quite s her.

What was it about her that made him so crazy? Sure, she was pretty. A knockout, really, with those long runner's legs and perfectly proportioned body. And her hands. They were strong, capable looking, and she had this way of lifting her fingertips to her face or brow as she spoke, making him want that featherlight touch on his own skin.

She'd drawn him in, wrapped him around those same fingers until, in that first crazy moment when he'd walked into the safe house and seen her, she could've had him with a single finger-crook.

Something had to give. Starting now. Tonight. He had to find a way to purge her from his system, a way to convince himself once and for all that he had to stay away from her, had to keep his hands to himself.

Either that or he had to have her.

JESSICA ANDERSEN

TWIN TARGETS

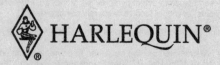

HARLEQUIN®

TORONTO • NEW YORK • LONDON
AMSTERDAM • PARIS • SYDNEY • HAMBURG
STOCKHOLM • ATHENS • TOKYO • MILAN • MADRID
PRAGUE • WARSAW • BUDAPEST • AUCKLAND

ISBN-13: 978-0-373-69328-3
ISBN-10:   0-373-69328-1

TWIN TARGETS

ABOUT THE AUTHOR

Though she's tried out professions ranging from cleaning sea lion cages to cloning glaucoma genes, from patent law to training horses, Jessica is happiest when she's combining all these interests with her first love: writing romances. These days she's delighted to be writing full-time on a farm in rural Connecticut that she shares with a small menagerie and a hero named Brian. She hopes you'll visit her at www.JessicaAndersen.com for info on upcoming books, contests and to say "hi"!

Books by Jessica Andersen

CAST OF CHARACTERS

Special Agent John Sharpe—Known as the Iceman, cold logic dictates every aspect of his work as leader of the FBI's major crimes unit. But when he goes up against one of the biggest bioweapons distributors in the world and a lovely scientist gets caught in the crossfire, cold logic clashes with fiery lust.

Sydney Westlake—Though she sometimes bends the rules to suit her own ends, the microbiologist never thought that trying to cure her sister's debilitating disease would put her on the path to developing a virus that could be used to undermine the very basis of DNA fingerprinting.

Tiberius—He might look like a college professor, but the evil genius is really all businessman, developing the most cutting-edge bioweapons and selling them to the highest bidder.

Celeste Westlake—Sydney's sister warned her not to work for a man like Tiberius.

Grace Mears—Sharpe's primary computer specialist is privy to the highest-level information within the team. But there's a leak within the major crimes unit. Does she serve another master?

Jimmy Oliverra—Grace's assistant has a wry sense of humor and the status of self-proclaimed geek.

Drew Dietz— The unit's evidence specialist keeps his own counsel.

Michael Pelotti—Sharpe's closest friend, the sharpshooter knows him better than anyone... and knows the secrets he keeps close.

Chapter One

Sydney Westlake made her move a half hour before the shift change, when the armed men who guarded the compound on Rocky Cliff Island would be at their least vigilant.

She hoped.

Tiberius was too smart to have a clockwork-regular schedule for something as important as security, so the armed forces that guarded the mansion and surrounding grounds worked randomly staggered shifts. After eleven months on the island, though—three of them as a prisoner—Sydney had found patterns in the randomness.

Today they were on what she'd dubbed "Schedule C," which meant the guard post located directly between her quarters and the boat dock would change shifts at 1:40 a.m. God willing.

"You can do this," she said to herself. "You *have* to do this. For Celeste." Her sister's name had become a mantra, something she held on to when her bravery faltered.

At first Sydney had told herself she was helping her ailing twin by staying on the island off the Massachusetts coast and working for Tiberius. She'd been trying to find a cure for the insidious genetic condition that was slowly killing Celeste. The obscenely large income being funneled into an offshore account was an added draw, allowing Celeste to stay in their wheelchair-friendly, restored Victorian in Maryland with a personal aide, rather than moving to an assisted-living facility of some sort. It had all seemed like a godsend when Tiberius first contacted her through his figurehead company, Tiberius Corp.

Now, though, she knew better. Tiberius wasn't a philanthropist and he wasn't a visionary. He was a monster, a sociopath, a self-professed businessman who wanted to use her discovery to do terrible things. Or rather, sell it to other criminals, who would use it as a smokescreen, hiding their identities while they did God only knew what.

She had to stop it from happening.

Trying not to betray her nerves, she crossed the high-tech lab Tiberius had ordered built and outfitted to her precise specifications. When she'd first arrived, the huge room, filled with the latest cutting-edge biotech equipment and analytical devices, had seemed like paradise. Now, it was a prison.

Sitting down at the bank of a half dozen networked computers, each of which controlled several of the big machines and analyzed the resulting data, she tried to block awareness of the security cameras blanketing the huge room, tried not to think about the men who were undoubtedly watching her image on-screen.

She'd done her prep work well. They'd gotten used

to her returning to the lab around 10:00 p.m. and working until one or so in the morning. If she were lucky, all they would see now was their tame lab rat pulling up the last set of results and then powering down the big machines for the night.

In reality, she was executing two programs she'd managed to sneak onto the island. One was an un-crackable lockdown program that would freeze all of the lab computers and machines until she typed in a password. The other would shut down all of the net-worked computers on Rocky Cliff Island—including the ones running power and security—for the space of five minutes, and then go back into hiding, supposedly untraceable by all but the original programmer.

Celeste had developed the routines just before she'd gotten sick; she was the techie, Sydney the bio-geek. Together, they'd used to joke, they were a nerd superhero.

Now, those powers would be put to the test.

"Okay, kids, do your thing." Sydney powered the lab computer down right after she'd fed the programs into the network. In ten minutes, the lights should go out. Then, the next time someone turned on one of the lab computers, the only thing they'd see on the screen would be a text prompt that read: Password?

If she made it off Rocky Cliff Island, she would use the password as leverage to keep her and Celeste alive long enough to grab the money out of her accounts and disappear. Then and only then, she would contact the au-thorities and tell them about Tiberius's plans.

If she died trying to escape, she could only hope Tiberius or his tech experts would try three wrong passwords, whereupon the worm would corrupt every piece of data on the network and fry the computers.

If she lived and was recaptured, though…

She shuddered. She'd seen what happened to people who crossed Tiberius. The image of what he'd done to Jenny Marie, the softhearted cook he'd caught sneaking e-mails between Sydney and Celeste, would remain burned on Sydney's retinas until the day she died. Unfortunately that day could be far sooner than she hoped, because crossing Tiberius was her only option right now. She couldn't allow him to use her scientific discovery for the purpose he intended; she had to stop him. Which meant it was now or never.

Sydney's fingers trembled as she hung her lab coat on its hook near the airlock-type passageway that was the only way in or out of the windowless lab. After pushing through the first of the pressurized doors, she touched the intercom button beside the second. "Out, please."

She'd long ago learned not to bother making small talk with the guards—it only made them suspicious. Nowadays, she stuck to her routine and they stuck to theirs, little suspecting that she was studying them and waiting for her chance to escape. Or maybe they'd suspected all along, and she was doomed before she even began.

The door unlocked with a click. Sydney held her breath as it swung open automatically, then exhaled in relief when she saw the hallway was empty. If they'd sent an escort she would've had to scrap her plan, but the armed escorts had gotten fewer and further between with every week and month she behaved herself, as she'd pretended to cooperate with Tiberius and his mad plan.

Forcing herself to breathe evenly, she stepped out into the hallway and headed for her quarters, trying to look like all she had on her mind was a few hours of sleep. When she reached the gray, featureless door leading to her two-room suite, she pressed another intercom button. "In, please."

The door clicked and opened, but instead of entering, she reached around the corner and fumbled for the thin wire she'd installed in the wall panel earlier that day, in the ten minutes she'd bought by "accidentally" blocking the view of the single camera in the main room of her suite by hanging a towel over the lens. By the time one of the guards had buzzed himself in without knocking, removed the offending item and groused at her for her continued sloppiness—which she'd carefully cultivated over the past few months—she'd done what needed to be done with the circuitry.

Concealed alongside the molding, the wire led to a simple gadget she'd Mickey Moused out of parts filched from the lab, using the diagram Celeste had sent via Jenny Marie. A sharp tug would form a bridge between the two main power lines in the wall beside the door, creating an obvious short and giving Tiberius's engineers no reason to look further for the source of the electrical failure.

At least that was the theory.

"Here goes nothing," she whispered, heart pounding. She checked her watch. Nine minutes fifty-five since she'd fed the kill program into the network. Fifty-six. Fifty-seven. As the door to her room started to close on its soundless mechanism, she yanked on the wire and jumped back.

There was a sizzle and a blinding flash in her room. Two seconds later the lights went out in the hallway, plunging her into utter blackness.

Sydney didn't think. She ran.

She heard muffled shouts and pounding feet as she bolted along the hallway and slammed through the door at the end, where she'd jimmied the lock earlier that day.

She was out!

The night was cold and rainy, which she hadn't anticipated. Sucking in a lungful of the wet, cutting air of springtime off the Atlantic coast, she plunged down a short cement staircase and bolted past a tarped-over swimming pool. Taking the direct route she'd mapped out during her daily guard-escorted walks around the compound, she headed for the dock at the bottom of the hill. The boats were little more than a collection of shadows against a misty backdrop of rain, dark against darker in the moonless, drizzly night.

She was halfway there when the backup generators kicked in, circumventing the primary network she'd crashed. Emergency lights flared to life and alarms whooped, the noise seeming to come from nowhere and everywhere at once.

Heart pounding, legs shaking with fear and adrenaline, Sydney ran for her life.

The drizzle had slicked everything with a thin layer of water, making the cement walkway slippery beneath her sneakers. The sharp wind cut through the jeans and light turtleneck shirt she'd worn in the climate-controlled lab. She hadn't dared trigger the guards' suspicions by dressing more heavily than that, and she paid for it as she pounded down a short incline to the water. Her teeth were chattering by the time she reached the first boat.

"Stop!" a voice shouted from behind her. Booted footsteps approached from the side at a run as the guards surrounded her. Gunfire chattered, kicking up stinging pellets of concrete directly ahead and to both sides of her.

They weren't aiming to kill. Not yet, anyway.

Ignoring the warning shots, Sydney took two running steps across the dock and flung herself toward the nearest motorboat, which was one of the small, fast two-seaters the guards used for shoreline patrols. She untied the craft from the dock and clambered aboard, ducking with a terrified scream as bullets smacked into the side of the boat and peppered the interior of the craft.

Her heart rocketed in her chest and for a split second she wanted to give up, wanted to put her hands up and say, "You win, I was just kidding. Take me back to the lab."

But she didn't. She couldn't. Still, her fingers shook as she punched the ignition button—her complacence had made the guards sloppy enough to leave the console unlocked, thank God—and the engine roared to life.

Coming from the other side of the island, past the cliff-side mansion, she heard the rotor thumps of Tiberius's helicopter preparing to lift off. She wasn't sure if he was evacuating or coming after her, but the sound added to the chaos of siren whoops and shouts as a dozen guards hit the dock, running flat out toward the other boats. The gunfire was silent for the moment, though, indicating that the security detail had orders to recapture her, not kill her.

She'd figured Tiberius would consider her far more of an asset than a liability…at least until it looked like she was going to succeed in escaping. Then he'd have his men start shooting for real.

Thank God for the rain. It would give her a layer of covering fog, and hopefully spoil their aim. The idea of being shot at—of being *shot*—terrified her, but she couldn't turn back now.

She slapped the throttle forward, blessing the summer she and Celeste had spent with a foster family on Moose-head Lake, where they'd learned the basics of boating. The motorboat leapt forward, spraying the dock with a plume of water that made the guards shout and curse, sounds that were quickly lost beneath the roar of the motorboat engine and the growing thump of the helicopter.

Sydney glanced back, to where the mansion rose high on the crest of the island, a dark, hulking shadow that was barely visible in the fog. Then the chopper swung up and over the building. Its searchlights cut through the mist, and the bumps of rockets were clearly visible on either skid.

That gave Sydney her answer: Tiberius wasn't fleeing. The bastard was coming after her.

Trembling with terror and adrenaline, breath sobbing in her lungs, she sent the little boat west, toward where the shoreline of northern Massachusetts ought to be. She couldn't see any town lights through the wind-driven rain, which was coming down harder by the moment. The pellets stung her face and throat, quickly soaking through her light clothing and plastering the fabric to her skin.

"Come on," she chanted. "You can do it. You can beat him." She wasn't sure if she was talking to herself or the boat, but the mantra made her feel a little better.

She almost couldn't believe that she'd gotten this far. The Sydney Westlake of a year earlier hadn't been able to fight for her university job or her project funding, hadn't been able to stand up for herself in the face of her ex's smear campaign, which had been the lowest of low academic politics.

But somehow, somewhere, she'd become the sort of woman who could plan an escape and make it happen.

Unfortunately, she'd also become a criminal, because whether or not Tiberius had coerced her—and he sure as hell had—she'd been the one to create the DNA code he considered his ultimate retail offering. Now it was up to her to make sure he never got to sell or use the engineered virus.

As she sent the boat into the gloom and the sounds of pursuit faded, hope guttered in her chest, pressing tears into her throat. She began to believe—when she hadn't really believed before, no matter what she'd told herself—that she was really going to get out of this mess, that she and Celeste were going to be okay.

Then something splashed loudly behind her, followed by a hiss and the growing thump of helicopter rotors. She turned and froze in terror. The chopper was directly behind her, and there was a dark shape in the water, churning a white wake as it sped toward her. A torpedo.

Tiberius had apparently decided she was a liability.

No, she thought. *Impossible.* Then the searchlights pinned on the boat and the surrounding water, illuminating the plume of the deadly missile speeding toward her boat and proving that it wasn't impossible at all. She was dead if she didn't move, and move fast.

Screaming, Sydney flung herself into the sea. The shock of the cold saltwater drove the air from her lungs, but she didn't have time to take another breath. She didn't think. She dove and swam down and away from the boat, kicking and stroking for all she was worth.

Moments later, the world went orange and a booming shockwave of water slapped at her, tumbling her end over end, pummeling the breath from her lungs, dazing her and making her ears ring.

She hung motionless, utterly disoriented, feeling the thud of her heartbeat in her head, in her bones.

She was vaguely aware that she was rising toward the surface, and something inside her said that was a bad thing. She couldn't seem to make her arms or legs obey her commands, though. She could only drift, longing for air as the water around her grew warmer, or maybe she got colder, she wasn't sure.

This isn't good, she thought, but couldn't seem to get beyond the thought.

Then the heavy rumble of a boat engine cut through her daze, and her brain came back online with a jolt. Tiberius's guards had arrived! Panic flared through her, chasing away the lethargy of shock, and she struck out wildly in the direction she thought was "up." Moments later she breached the surface and sucked in a gasping lungful of air. Then she was swimming, flailing her arms and legs as hard as she could in an effort to get away from the motor noise as her heart hammered in her ears and panic spurred her on.

There was a splash behind her as at least one of the guards jumped in to grab her.

"No!" She swam harder, adrenaline propelling her onward when her muscles trembled with fear and fatigue, and the numbing cold of the water around her.

Her head pounded and there was a sharp pain above her eye, suggesting she'd been cut by waterborne debris. She banged into other pieces of debris as she swam, and the air was tainted with the odor of gasoline and smoke. She wanted to cough but she couldn't spare the breath as she swam for all she was worth. She had to get away, had to—

A hand closed on her ankle, gripped hard and dragged her under.

Panic jolted and she screamed, then inhaled water and choked hard. She thrashed, fighting her captor even as she struggled to the surface and gagged, trying to get the water out of her lungs, the air in. The world spun and closed in on her, and her captor shifted his grip from her leg to her throat, clamping an arm across her upper chest while he struck out, swimming strongly with his free arm and kicks from his powerful legs.

"Let me go!" Sydney struggled against him, fouling his rhythm and dragging them both below, but he didn't fight. He simply waited until they broke the surface, then shifted his arm to her throat and squeezed until her world went gray and spun to a pinprick.

Semiconscious, she went limp against him, barely breathing even after he eased up on the choke hold. Defeat hammered through her, alongside the sure knowledge of what Tiberius would do to her now.

He wasn't just going to kill her. He was going to force

her to help him sell a terrible opportunity to terrible people. Then he was going to kill her and Celeste both, very slowly. That was what he'd promised he'd do if she betrayed him, and she had every reason to believe the threat. She was going to die, and die horribly.

The realization spurred her to a last desperate attempt to escape. Knowing she had just one more chance, she waited until her captor reached the slick white side of a tall boat and called for others to reach down and grab her. At the moment he handed her off, she found another burst of energy and exploded, kicking and scratching at the two men who held her. They cursed and fought to hang on to her. They shouted at her, but she was too far gone to process the words.

She screamed over and over again until her voice went raw and then broke to sobs as they subdued her by grabbing her arms and legs and hanging on despite her furious struggles. When she finally went limp, they dragged her up and over the side, and dumped her onto the rain-slicked deck.

Moments later, the man who'd jumped in after her landed on the deck nearby, dripping and breathing hard.

Sydney curled herself into a protective ball, waiting for rough hands to tie her so she couldn't get away while they hauled her back to her quarters on the island—or worse, directly to Tiberius.

Instead of rope, though, a heavy wool blanket landed atop her, cutting the sting of the cold air.

She whimpered and clutched at the blanket, pulling it over her head. After a minute or two, when the warmth started to come and the men hadn't made another move, she peered out, dragging the blanket around herself as she struggled partway up on the rain-slicked deck.

Her teeth were chattering and her dark, shoulder-length hair was plastered over her forehead, covering her eyes. She slicked the strands away from her face, and when her vision cleared, she found herself only a few feet away from the man who'd pulled her from the ocean.

He was leaning back against the side of the gunwale a few feet away from her, wearing a coarse gray blanket like hers. His wet hair was short and dark, his features square and regular, his blue eyes assessing. Even soaking wet, he carried a definite aura of command.

She didn't recognize him, but that didn't mean anything. She'd only seen a few of Tiberius's guards face-to-face, but had heard the footsteps of many more. What was strange, though, was that he was looking at her with utter calm, laced with an air of speculation. He seemed willing to wait for her to speak first, which didn't make any sense.

Then her eyes locked on his blanket, which had something written on it in six-inch-high letters: U.S. Coast Gu—

It broke off where he'd tucked one side of the blanket beneath the other, but it was enough to have hope blooming viciously in her chest.

She hadn't been recaptured after all.

She'd been rescued!

She gasped and looked at the other two men standing nearby. They were burly, curly-haired guys with the shared features of brothers and coast guard insignias on their jackets.

When she looked back at the man who'd saved her, he nodded in greeting, but didn't smile. "I'm Special Agent John Sharpe of the FBI's major crimes task force, and you're on the coast guard cutter *Valiant*." He paused, expression assessing. "Whether that's good or bad news for you is going to depend on what you were doing on Rocky Cliff Island and why Tiberius wants you dead."

Chapter Two

John stood, draping the blanket over his shoulders to stave off the sharp wind, and looked down at the woman who huddled miserably on the deck. The drowned-rat factor did little to hide her high, angular cheekbones or delicately tipped-up nose, or the exotic tilt to her chocolate-brown eyes.

She was, in a word, gorgeous.

He had no clue whether she'd been Tiberius's prisoner or a coconspirator gone bad, but her looks alone made him lean in the latter direction, because he'd seen the file photos of the bastard's previous women and she certainly fit the type.

Still, there was no need to head straight for "bad cop" interrogation techniques. For now, he'd let her see him as the rescuer, willing to play along with whatever game she had in mind. With Tiberius and his people it was all about the game, John knew. Move and countermove. A living chess match, played out on a continent-size board, with living people as the pieces and national security the stakes.

Not yet sure whether she was a pawn or a queen or

somewhere in between, he held out a hand to help her up. "Come on. I don't know about you, but I could use some coffee, a few towels and some dry clothes."

She stared at him, her lovely brown eyes stark in her pale face. Her hand trembled when she reached for his, making him think either she was a damn good actress sent to put him off his game, or else she'd truly been running for her life. Maybe she'd double-crossed Tiberius, John mused, or maybe he'd simply grown tired of her and didn't want any loose ends returning to the mainland.

Those thoughts died quickly, though, because the moment he and the woman linked hands and he pulled her to her feet, she burst into tears.

"Oh, hell," he said. "Please don't cry." He didn't do tears.

Instead of stopping, she buried her face in her free hand and sobbed harder, her shoulders—her whole body, for that matter—shaking with reaction…or a good approximation of it.

Reminding himself he was supposed to be playing along with the illusion of a damsel in distress, John grimaced and put an arm around her in a stiff offer of comfort. He patted her shoulder. "You're safe. It's over."

She turned into him, wrapped her arms around his waist and hung on as though she never meant to let go. "Thank you," she whispered against his neck, her skin warming against his despite the chill. *"Thank you."*

Electricity jolted through him in a surge of reaction that was so unexpected, it literally took his breath away. Heat flared and his heart did a thumpity-thump number that set up a clamor of warning bells.

Damn, she was good. Lucky for him, he'd had practice with this sort of thing, and he'd learned his lesson the hard way.

Besides, they didn't call him Iceman because he was warm and fuzzy.

"It's okay," he said, trying to disengage without making it into a wrestling match. He fleetingly wished he'd brought Grace Mears along on this run, or sharpshooter Michael Pelotti, both of whom were way better than he at comforting victims and witnesses—and suspects—while making it seem natural. Hell, pretty much anyone on his team had him beat at this sort of thing.

He looked at the coast guarders. "Can one of you help me out here?"

Dick and Doug Renfrew, the boat handlers he'd borrowed for the night's surveillance, shook their heads in unison. "Not unless you want to hang around and wait for the chopper to make another pass," Doug said. He was the talker of the two.

"Good point," John said, glancing at the gray-black sky. "You should probably get us the hell out of here."

Granted, Tiberius's helicopter had peeled off into the fog when it saw the U.S.C.G. ship approaching the scene of the explosion, and he'd heard the other motorboats cut and head back to the island, but they could swing back around for a second look at any moment.

Tiberius and his crew had probably assumed the *Valiant* was fully manned and ready to act, but the reality was that the cutter was carrying its minimum crew of two, along with one senior FBI agent—John—

who was acting on a hunch that hadn't even been strong enough to justify bringing along the rest of his team.

His gut told him Tiberius was gearing up for something big, something that was focused on his private island off the New England coast. Based on that, he'd called in a few favors and gone on a semiofficial fishing expedition off the fertile ledges of George's Bank.

The good news was that he'd caught something. The bad news was that he wasn't sure exactly what he'd caught.

Tiberius was smart enough—and devious enough—to have seen the *Valiant* on his surveillance systems, identified it through its transponder code and sent one of his people out to get herself "captured" as a diversion. It would be just like him to feed the FBI a decoy intended to distract them away from his main intent.

The question was: had he?

John looked down at the woman, who was quieting some, though she stayed leaning against him as though she found the contact as comforting as he found it disturbing.

"Come on," he said, voice unaccountably rough. "Let's get you warmed up, Ms...." He let the sentence trail off in a prompt.

"Sydney," she said against his chest. "Just Sydney." Which could either mean she figured they should be on a first-name basis after what they'd just been through together, or that she didn't intend to voluntarily give him enough to figure out who she was for real.

He didn't recognize her name or face from the extensive files Grace and Jimmy Oliverra—the two computer jocks on his team—had amassed on Tiberius and his dealings, but that didn't mean she wasn't part of his world. Just that she hadn't said "cheese" yet and gotten her picture taken for the FBI's scrapbook.

"Okay, just Sydney," he said, playing the game. "Let's get you belowdecks, out of this wind." He disengaged and gestured her across the rain-slicked deck to the ladder that led to the cramped galley and sitting area downstairs.

She fumbled slightly when the boat sliced deeper into the storm and the chop increased. But she looked steady enough overall, as if she wasn't going to collapse again. Was it part of an act or was it reality?

John didn't know, but he sure as hell intended to find out, ASAP.

"You can go straight on through," he said when she paused in a short hallway. "The head is to your right. There's no shower, but if you want to get out of those wet clothes and towel yourself off, I'll scrounge something for you to wear. There's a first-aid kit under the sink. When you're changed, I'll meet you in the galley. I'll fix us some coffee." *With a side of interrogation.*

She was pretty out of it, between shock and the gash on her forehead, but he didn't feel the slightest bit of remorse about questioning her. Experience had taught him that the things people in her condition said were usually more truthful than what came out of their mouths after they'd had a chance to think about their answers. And if that made him the cold, cynical SOB his teammates claimed, then so be it. His suspicious nature had kept him alive when plenty of others around him—good men and women—had died in their efforts to take down the kingpins of modern organized crime.

These days, the major crimes unit wasn't about territories or ethnicity, it was all about technology. The modern godfathers controlled pieces of science and sold them to the highest bidders…and Tiberius was king among the black market tech dealers.

Tiberius didn't have a last name that any intelligence service worldwide had been able to find, never mind a history prior to ten years ago, when he'd appeared on the scene almost overnight. He was the worst among the worst, dealing almost exclusively in microscopic weaponry of the germ warfare variety. He'd been variously blamed for bioweapons attacks on five of the seven continents, including targeted viral assassinations in Europe and the U.S., and a series of flulike epidemic outbreaks along the conflict fronts in the Middle East.

Tiberius was bad news, there was no doubt about it. Unfortunately, he'd proved all but untouchable over the decade he'd been in business. There was no solid evidence connecting him directly to any crime and nobody would testify against him—at least not anyone who'd managed to stay alive long enough to take the witness stand. The calculating bastard lived sequestered on his private island off the Massachusetts coast when he could've been someplace warm and inviting and outside of U.S. soil. John was convinced he'd chosen Rocky Cliff Island for spite, so he could laugh at the agents who'd dedicated—and given—their lives in a series of unsuccessful efforts to put him behind bars.

Unsuccessful until now, that is, he thought as he dug through a spare clothes locker, changed into jeans, a U.S.C.G. sweatshirt and thick socks, and grabbed a slightly smaller set of the same for his mysterious guest.

Sydney—if that was really her name at all—might just be the answer to his prayers. Though his gut told him she'd probably been Tiberius's lover, he'd just tried to kill her. That might be all the leverage John and his people would need to get inside information.

Then again, she could be a clever plant. The possibility meant he'd have to be very, very careful in what he said and did around her.

He knocked on the door to the head. "There's a set of clothes for you outside the door. I'll be in the galley when you're ready."

A couple of minutes later, right about when the small kitchen space had started to take on the aroma of hot coffee, the door to the washroom opened and Sydney stepped out.

Her towel-dried brunette hair stuck up in tufts here and there, suggesting it would curl later. The borrowed clothes hung off her slight frame, and she'd cuffed the jeans so they wouldn't drag on the ground. She should've looked ridiculous in the too-large pants and sweatshirt. The fact that she didn't, that she somehow looked as though a fashion designer had chosen the outfit and told her to make it work on the runway, had those warning buzzers going off again in the back of John's brain, loud and clear.

He stared at her, seeing a drop-dead gorgeous woman beneath shock and saltwater, and thought, *Were you his lover? A customer in a deal gone bad? Are you a victim, a perp, or somewhere in between?*

As if he'd said the question aloud, she locked eyes with him. "So, Special Agent John Sharpe of the FBI... are you authorized to make a deal?"

SYDNEY SAW THE mental shields come crashing down. One minute he'd been looking at her as though trying to make up his mind about her, and in the next she'd made it for him, because innocent people don't need deals.

His gorgeous blue eyes blanked and a small, sardonic smile touched the corners of his lips, which were bracketed with small creases that drew her eyes and made her wonder what he'd look like if he smiled—really smiled—at her.

"It depends on what you're offering," he said, expression giving away nothing.

She wanted to tell him that she intended to give him everything she knew, that she couldn't live with herself if Tiberius got away with what he was planning. But she had to be realistic. All she knew about this guy was that he was an FBI agent—she figured she could believe that much, because she highly doubted the coast guard loaned their boats and crew to just anyone. Well, she also knew he'd dried off even handsomer than she'd expected. That wasn't exactly relevant, but it was certainly a fact.

His hair was a rich, dark brown, thick and wavy. From his square-jawed features and the stress lines carved beside his mouth, she guessed he was in his mid-thirties, a few years older than she. Wearing a gray coast guard sweatshirt, borrowed jeans and thick socks—as she was—he should've looked casual. Instead, he exuded that same leadership she'd noticed out on the deck, that same "don't mess with me" attitude.

On one level she found it comforting. On another, disturbing.

She'd known men like him before, men who would

do—and say—anything necessary to achieve their goals if they thought the ends justified the means. Hell, she'd dated one of them—almost been engaged to him—and look where that had gotten her: unemployed and forced to seek an alternative source of funding that had turned out to be far less legitimate than she'd hoped.

Thankfully, this time forewarned is forearmed, she thought grimly.

No doubt Agent Sharpe figured that the end of bringing down a man like Tiberius would justify any means. She, on the other hand, needed to protect not only herself, but also Celeste. To do that, she had to maintain whatever leverage she could get her hands on.

Knowing it, steeling herself to negotiate when her conscience was crying for her to spill every last piece of information on the spot, she stayed silent, waiting for Sharpe to start the negotiations.

Instead, he handed her a cup of coffee and gestured her to the small dining area of the galley, where there was a booth-style table and bench seats.

She sat, blew across the surface of the steaming liquid and took a small sip, welcoming the burn of heat and the bite of caffeine.

He sat down opposite her, and the booth was so cramped that their knees bumped beneath the table while he got himself settled. She moved away, all too aware of his maleness, of the way his aura filled the small space and made her think of how long she'd gone without a man's touch.

Swallowing through a suddenly tight throat and reminding herself that she needed to tread carefully, she lifted her coffee mug and said, "You'll find me in the system as soon as you run the prints off this mug—presuming, of course, that's your plan if I haven't told you who I am before we reach the U.S.C.G. station at Gloucester."

She expected the obvious question: *why are your prints on file?* Instead, he skipped right over that and said, "In other words, you needed government clearance at some point."

She raised an eyebrow, then winced when the motion pulled at the cut she'd cleaned and bandaged in the bathroom. "You're assuming I wasn't arrested."

Again, his smile held no humor. "Consider it a hunch, based on what I know of Tiberius's women."

"I wasn't his lover." There was little heat in the denial, though she was tempted to ask why that had been his first guess. She wondered how he saw her, what she looked like to him.

After almost a year of interacting solely with the guards and Tiberius's people, it seemed suddenly strange to be speaking with a man—a tongue-draggingly handsome man—who wasn't part of that world.

But that was the point, wasn't it? He wasn't entirely out of that world—he was simply on the other side. She wasn't sure she could trust John Sharpe. She'd trusted Tiberius, and that hadn't turned out well at all.

"But you're right that I haven't been arrested," she conceded his point. "A few parking tickets and a stern warning for doing sixty in a thirty-five zone outside Bethesda, but that's it. And yes, I needed government clearance." She paused, trying to gauge how much to reveal, how much to hold back. Finally, she went with what she figured he could get from her prints and a quick background check. "My name is Sydney Westlake. I'm twenty-eight, my twin sister, Celeste, and I were raised together in foster care and we own a house together in Glen Hills, Maryland. Up until a year ago, I worked in the genetics department of the Advanced Institute of Science in Bethesda, investigating the causes and possible cures for a rare genetic disease called Singer's syndrome."

She paused when the boat's engine note changed and their momentum slowed. There were no windows in the small galley, but she thought she heard the clang of a marker buoy, indicating that they were nearing land.

"What changed a year ago?" Sharpe prompted.

"As you might guess from the fact that I was swimming like hell to get away from Rocky Cliff Island," she said drily, "I went to work for Tiberius. About a year ago my funding was cut, thanks to my lying rat-bastard of an ex-boyfriend. A few weeks after that happened, a representative of the Tiberius Corporation made me an offer I couldn't refuse. I've been working in a private lab on the island ever since, the last three months of it under lock and key until tonight."

He'd gone completely and utterly still as she spoke, making her think of a predator freezing the moment it sighted prey. His voice was inflectionless—and damning—when he said, "You developed bioweapons."

She wanted to flinch from the condemnation, but didn't because it was the truth. A far more complicated truth than he made it sound, but the truth nonetheless.

"Not intentionally, and not willingly once I figured out what he actually wanted me to do…but yes, ultimately I developed a new DNA-based vector for Tiberius, and yes, under certain circumstances, it could be used for illegal purposes."

She couldn't quite bring herself to call it a bioweapon. It should've been a cure, a salvation. Instead, it was a direct threat to national security.

Sharpe set his coffee aside, very deliberately, and folded his hands on the table. "What is the target? How long do we have?"

Incongruously, she noticed that he wasn't wearing a wedding ring. Even more unsettlingly, she found that she was glad.

It's only because he's the first male nonfelon you've seen in eleven-plus months, she told herself. That, and she appreciated how he'd stayed one jump ahead of her in their conversation. He didn't repeat himself, and didn't fill the air with useless questions and chatter. He was cool and calculating, yes, but she could already tell he was extremely intelligent.

Which could make him very dangerous. He was smart, he had an agenda and he had the law on his side. It was up to her to make sure she got what she needed without pushing so far that she got herself locked up, leaving Celeste unprotected when Tiberius came for her. Because he *would* come for her. There was no question of that.

Even now, the need to get to her ailing twin sister beat beneath Sydney's skin, along with the fear that the time taken up with her rescue and the boat ride had been too long, that Tiberius would have already figured out what Sydney had done before she left.

If she were in his position she'd grab whatever her adversary held dear, demand the computer password in exchange and then disappear with the technology.

Since this was Tiberius they were talking about, he would probably do exactly that…and then once he had the password, he'd kill her and Celeste outright because she'd dared to cross him.

"Sydney, how long do we have until he sells whatever you developed?" Sharpe pressed.

"You have some time," she answered. "I corrupted the lab reagents and jammed the computers on the way out. Without the password, it'll take another scientist weeks, maybe months to re-create what I did. With the password…" She trailed off, trying not to consider that possibility but knowing she had to. "With the password, he could be up and running in a few days. Maybe less."

He muttered a curse as the boat engines cut out and the craft drifted for a few seconds, then bumped up against the dock. Above decks, they could hear the sound of tramping footsteps and men's shouts as coast guard crewmen fastened the lines and secured the cutter.

"And the target?" Sharpe asked.

Sydney kept her eyes on his, refusing to look away even though she wanted to hide her head and pretend it was all a nightmare, that she hadn't really handed this sort of power to a man like Tiberius. "The eventual target is, indirectly, the entire United States legal system."

"Go on."

Telling herself this was the only way, Sydney said,

"I built a viral vector that was intended to treat the effects of Singer's syndrome. Under orders—threats, really—from Tiberius, I altered the vector so it mimics the twenty marker sequences currently used for a standard DNA fingerprinting profile." She paused, saw from his dark expression that he got it, and nodded. "Exactly. Once someone has been infected with the viral vector, any samples coming from his or her body will yield incomprehensible blurs with standard forensic DNA analysis. The police labs will be completely unable to match his—or her—DNA to crime scene samples or DNA fingerprints already on file."

He muttered a low, vicious oath. "In other words, you've single-handedly given one of the most ruthless criminal businessmen on the planet the power to render the CODIS DNA database—and a good chunk of modern forensic analysis—completely useless."

Now she did look away. "It's pointless to say how sorry I am. I thought the job was a legit front for his other dealings. I thought I could use his money—use him—to help people." To help Celeste, and others like her who were often overlooked in favor of efforts to cure more common—and therefore more commercially lucrative—diseases.

"You're smarter than that," he said without inflection, and for some reason that stung more than all the names she'd called herself in the dark of night back on the island, when she'd realized exactly the same thing.

She wasn't just smart enough to know better, she *had* known better and she'd taken the job anyway, because she'd been so desperate to find a way to help

Celeste, so obsessed with the goal of prolonging her sister's life and making up for the fact that the disease had struck one of them but not the other.

As Celeste had accused her on more than one occasion, she'd been so sure she was right, she'd bent the rules to get what she wanted.

Sharpe focused on her, his eyes gone dark with accusation, with condemnation. "Tell me more, and tell me fast. I'll need you to reproduce whatever you can remember about the vector and your work so I can kick it over to the Centers for Disease Control and Homeland Security and get them started on a counter-agent. Then you're going to sit down with me and the rest of my team, and we're going to go over the past year of your life step by step. You're going to tell me everything you can remember about the setup on the island." He paused. "Basically, your butt is mine starting now, until I say otherwise. When it's all over, if I'm satisfied that you've cooperated fully, then we'll talk about your culpability and possible charges."

Sydney was surprised and not a little dismayed to realize that the slap of scorn in his voice mattered to her, that his opinion mattered when it absolutely, positively shouldn't. He was a means to an end, nothing more.

Still, she couldn't help wishing they'd met under different circumstances, maybe even during different lifetimes. She thought she would've enjoyed getting to know John Sharpe a bit better, and figuring out what went on behind those cool blue eyes. Unfortunately, under these circumstances in this lifetime, they were destined to be at odds.

She cemented that by standing and taking the two

steps needed to bring her into his personal space, then looking down at him. "I'm sorry, but that's not how it's going to work, Agent Sharpe."

He narrowed his eyes. "Excuse me?"

Reminding herself not to back off, not to back away, she inhaled a breath that contained entirely too much of his energy, and said, "This is where the deal part comes in. I'll tell you everything I know, but in exchange, I want guaranteed immunity from federal prosecution no matter what happens, and I want my sister and me placed in protective custody, effective immediately." She faltered a little. "Tiberius is going to try to get to me through her. I can absolutely, positively promise that."

Sharpe rose from the booth and looked down at her for a long moment, his eyes seeming to pierce deep inside her and see things she'd rather keep hidden. She expected more questions, and braced herself to remain mute until she had a lawyer and a signed agreement, and assurances that Celeste was safe.

She was surprised when he said only, "You disappoint me."

Then he turned and strode from the small room, his angry strides far too big for the tiny space.

When he was gone, leaving his energy to vibrate into nothingness, Sydney remained staring after him. "Yeah," she finally said, pressing a hand to her churning stomach. "I disappoint myself, too. The thing is, I'm doing my best to fix it."

Unfortunately, she didn't think he saw it that way, which made him dangerous. *Watch yourself with that one,* she told herself as she headed for the narrow ladder. *He's too smart, too sure of himself.*

If she wasn't careful, Special Agent John Sharpe could ruin everything.

Chapter Three

John knew he shouldn't have been surprised by what Sydney had revealed. And he wasn't really. What surprised him was the depth of his anger. She might not have been Tiberius's lover, but what she *had* done was far worse.

He'd wanted her to be innocent, he realized as they disembarked and slogged their way toward the main building of the coast guard station. Despite the fact that he damn well knew better, he'd wanted her to be innocent, which she so incredibly wasn't.

"Can I borrow your phone?" she said suddenly.

He handed it over. "Calling your lawyer?"

She sent him a look that he couldn't interpret, but that touched his skin with a skitter of warning, of want. She said softly, "Do you blame me?"

She dialed a Maryland exchange, waking what sounded from her side of the conversation like the lawyer who'd been handling her affairs while she'd been on Rocky Cliff Island. He referred her to someone local and she made a second call.

Within fifteen minutes, a fifty-ish briefcase-toting

blond woman in a mint-green skirt suit strode through the front door of the coast guard station, looking wide-awake even though it was nearly 3:00 a.m.

John watched her eyes skim the room and could practically see her thought process as she sorted through the coast guarders and himself before reaching Sydney: *pilot, pilot, swimmer, cop, ah—client.*

She made a beeline for Sydney, took up a protective position at her client's side and then turned to John, having apparently—and erroneously, at least at the C.G. station—identified him as the guy in charge. "Is there somewhere private my client and I can speak?" the lawyer asked.

John gestured to a nearby door, having already cleared it through the Renfrew brothers and their superiors. "You can borrow that office. My people are pulling together the paperwork as we speak."

Sydney looked at him, and he caught a flash of nerves and worry in her lovely brown eyes. "What about my sister?"

"The locals are already en route. They'll make sure she's safe and get her someplace protected." He'd thought briefly about using the sister as leverage, but had decided against it, not because he had any compunction against using the tools given to him, but because he knew Tiberius well enough to realize the good guys would lose that leverage if they delayed.

Instead of looking relieved, she looked discomfited, and a little guilty. "You'll need…" She trailed off, took a breath and said, "Celeste is wheelchair-bound and requires special care. You'll need to take her care provider with her, or find someone else to do the job, and you'll need a vehicle she can be wheeled onto. She shouldn't be removed from the chair."

Only his natural tendency to play his cards close to his chest kept John from cursing, not only because it meant reorganizing what was supposed to be a quick find-and-grab, but also because it proved what he'd already begun to suspect: Sydney Westlake was planning on giving him exactly as much information as she chose to, exactly *when* she chose to. This wasn't a free exchange of information. It was a damn chess game.

Worse, he was finding himself intrigued by her rather than annoyed, which was surprising, and he didn't care for surprises. In his experience, they tended to end badly.

"Let me guess," he said as a few more pieces of the puzzle connected in his brain. "Your sister has Singer's syndrome."

"My twin sister. Yes."

"Which explains why you locked the computers instead of destroying them." If he'd been a cursing man he would've let rip right then, because the information added a whole new layer of complications with the realization that her goal and his weren't the same.

He wanted Tiberius dead or behind bars, and wasn't really picky which way it went as long as the bastard was out of circulation and his operation disassembled piece by miserable piece. She, on the other hand, wanted to save her sister with a treatment that could potentially be used to topple the federal justice system, and then get her life back without any repercussions.

"Yes," she agreed, glancing away from him. "The

computers were firewalled against connection to any outside network, so I couldn't e-mail the files off the island, and Tiberius's people wouldn't supply me with a flash drive or anything I could carry with me. I kept both my main and backup files on the system, and now they're locked until either you take down Tiberius and get me back on that island, or Tiberius tortures the password out of me."

She said the words with such hollow calm that he believed her, and even felt a stir of compassion. He, too, had seen what happened to people who wound up on the wrong side of Tiberius. It wasn't pretty.

"Look," he said, "I can sympathize to a degree. If I had a sister I'd probably feel the same way. But all the good intentions in the world don't change the fact that you went to the island willingly." His voice turned hard. "I might have to accept this deal, but I'll be damned if I let you withhold valuable information in the hopes of saving your sister. Getting our hands on—or destroying—the weapon you created is our first priority. Bringing Tiberius down is our second. I'm sorry, but recovering information that might or might not cure your sister has to come behind both of those things on my priority list."

He expected her to argue fiercely. Instead, she inclined her head ever so slightly. "I know." She blew out a breath and pressed her palm to her stomach beneath the borrowed sweatshirt. "In my head I know all that. I even told myself it would be okay if I died escaping, and Celeste died because I didn't make it out and get the cure to her, as long as Tiberius couldn't use my work the way he wants to." She paused, then shook her head. "The thing is, I'm not that person. Maybe it makes me selfish or spoiled, but I'm not willing to make that sacrifice." She fixed John with a look. "It's up to you, big guy. You take what I'm willing to give you and run with it, or I'm out of here the first chance I get, and then Celeste and I are off the radar."

He should've scoffed at the threat, but damned if he didn't think she could do it. She'd managed to lock down her work—though he had only her word on that one—and get off Rocky Cliff Island herself. Who was to say she couldn't grab her sister and disappear off the FBI's radar, as well?

His level of respect for her, which was already far too high considering they were on opposite sides of this particular issue, inched up another notch.

"Write up your terms." He gestured to the empty office. "I'll e-mail the info to my people and get the honchos to sign off on the deal." He fixed Sydney with a look. "Then you're going to tell me everything."

She turned away, but then paused and looked back, and her eyes were dark with regret. "We're on the same side, you know. I want Tiberius put away just as much as you do."

"I highly doubt that."

"I'm sorry," she said again, so quietly he almost didn't hear her.

Steeling himself against an unexpected—and unwelcome—surge of warmth, he said, "It doesn't matter whether we like each other or not, Ms. Westlake. I have something you want, you have something I want. Let's do the deal and take down Tiberius before he sells your virus to the wrong people and they use it to bring down CODIS. Once we've done that, you can get on with your life and I can get on with the next case. It's as simple as that."

But as he turned away, effectively ending the conversation, he knew damn well that none of this was going to be the slightest bit simple.

NERVES JANGLING in her stomach, Sydney followed her lawyer, Emily Breslow, into the office Sharpe had indicated.

She hated how her conversation with the agent had gone, hated having to play this game, but what other choice did she have?

"It's like I always say," Emily began, waving her to one of the two chairs, which faced each other across a cluttered desk in the untidy office, "if you have to deal with the Feds, it helps to deal with a cute one."

That startled a snort out of Sydney. Her new lawyer was nothing like she'd expected. Tom Dykstra, the guy in Bethesda she'd used to set up a living trust for Celeste, had fit her sober, cynical, suited-up image of a lawyer. Emily, not so much. Though she wore a suit, it was anything but sober, and even though it was the middle of the night—closing in on morning—she was wide-awake, and her eyes held a glint of humor, as though she might laugh at any moment.

She was also, according to Sydney's Maryland-based shark of a lawyer, very good at her job. And she had a point about it being a side bonus to work with a cute

Fed. The more time Sydney spent in the presence of John Sharpe, the more interesting he was getting.

"Agent Sharpe seems very…focused," Sydney said finally, though the word seemed entirely inadequate in describing the handsome, charismatic—and danger-ous—man she'd gotten herself tangled up with.

"He'd have to be." Emily dipped into her briefcase and pulled out a thin folder. "Here, sign this. Standard firm contract, yadda, yadda." While Sydney scanned the document, Emily continued, "I called in a few favors on the way over and got the scoop on Sharpe—what there is of it, anyway. He's thirty-five, no siblings, parents living abroad. The FBI recruited him straight out of Georgia Tech, where he was a star on both the football team and the chess club. Go figure."

When the words on the page blurred into legalese, Sydney blinked, trying to focus on the contract. Good business practice demanded that she read and dissect it line by line, but expediency—and a lack of other options—had her signing on the dotted line of duplicate copies after only a quick skim of the document.

Besides, even though she knew it shouldn't matter, she wanted to hear the rest of the story. "So he was a brainy jock," she said, prompting Emily.

"Still is, from the looks of it," the older woman said, but more with the air of a connoisseur than someone who wanted him for herself. She continued, "He made one of the quickest rises through the ranks ever seen, and is still fairly young to be heading up a unit. He has the reputation of being dedicated and driven, even ruthless sometimes, but everyone I talked to said that his word is good. He doesn't make a promise he doesn't intend to keep."

"In other words, you think I can trust him."

"Yes and no." The lawyer took one of the copies of the signed contract and tucked it into her briefcase, leaving the other in front of Sydney. "His team has an excellent record of bringing down major criminals, and their conviction record is solid. I think you can trust him to follow whatever deal he signs off on to the letter. However, that's the key—he'll do exactly what he's promised, and no more. Watch your back and don't assume anything about him or his motivations. You heard him out there. His job is to bring down Tiberius, not protect your work…and maybe not even protect you, if you get in his way."

"I'll keep that in mind," Sydney said, pressing a hand to her suddenly queasy stomach. "And may I say that I'm blown away by how much you managed to get on him in such a short time frame."

The lawyer grinned, and for the first time Sydney saw a flash of steel beneath the pleasant exterior. "Don't worry about the overtime. You're paying through the nose for my services."

"I'm sure I am," Sydney murmured, suddenly realizing how oddly normal it felt to be talking with another woman, someone who wasn't a guard or cook, or one of Tiberius's enforcers, or the boss himself. This was possibly the least normal situation she'd ever found herself in, yet the act of speaking with Emily felt so normal, it was nearly enough to bring her to tears, driving home how much she'd left behind when she left for Rocky Cliff Island, how much more she'd lost than she'd planned on or even realized.

How much more she might yet lose.

"Okay, that was a fun bit of get-to-know-the-players, but we have work to do." Emily pulled a slim laptop computer from her briefcase, set it on the desk and flipped open the flexible screen, turning it so they could both see the display. A few taps on the keyboard woke the machine from hibernation and pulled up a document, this one written in even denser legalese than the contract had been. "This is a pretty standard skeleton for a federal immunity deal, along with some language for witness protection, either through WITSEC or protective custody. Based on the particulars of your situation, I'm going to suggest that we—"

The door opened without a warning knock and Sharpe entered the room, filling it as much with his presence as his physical mass.

Sydney frowned, knowing she should be irritated with the interruption, but feeling something else instead, a little lift in the region of her heart, one that warned her she was well on her way to crushing on the agent, despite them being on opposite sides of too many issues.

He must've had clothes in his car, because he'd changed out of the borrowed sweats into a tailored navy suit with a crisp white shirt underneath, and a pair of oxblood shoes that were incongruously rubber soled, as though they were business shoes intended to double for foot pursuit—which they probably were. That detail, and the glimpse of a shoulder holster beneath his suit jacket, took the look from "upscale businessman" to something else entirely.

Something that sent a quiver of nerves—and heat—through her core.

Going for bravado, she started to ask if that was it for their privacy, but something in his cool blue eyes stopped her, making her ask instead, "What's wrong?"

"The local cops just reported in from your house in Maryland. Your sister is missing and her aide and the aide's boyfriend are dead."

Celeste missing. The others dead.

The words didn't make any sense.

Sydney sat for a second as her heart beat loud in her ears and her mind refused to process his blunt words. *Impossible,* she told herself. That sort of thing didn't happen in real life. Didn't happen to people like her and Celeste.

Except it did when she made the mistake of working for a monster like Tiberius, and then compounded the mistake by double-crossing him.

She rose on legs that threatened to buckle beneath her, and took the few steps necessary to bring her face-to-face with Sharpe. "Take me there."

"We're not finished here," Emily protested, but Sydney waved her off.

"You'll have to do the best you can without me. Call me if you have any questions. I'll give you my—" She broke off, realizing she'd canceled her cell phone before she left for the island. She had no phone and no money, and her ID and credit cards were locked up. She was nobody until she retrieved her life from the safe in her bedroom at home.

A home that had been violated. Where two people had been killed.

An image flashed into her mind, that of Jenny Marie's body after it had washed up on the beach down-current from Rocky Cliff. The cook's dark hair had been matted with seaweed and sand, and blue crabs had nibbled at her fingers, toes and eyes, but that hadn't been enough to disguise the horrible things Tiberius had done to her before he'd killed her and thrown her over the edge.

This, he'd been saying to Sydney with his actions. *This is what I'll do to you if you cross me. This is what I'll do to the people around you.* Like Jenny Marie.

Like Celeste.

Tears filmed Sydney's vision and a sob caught in her throat.

"Here." Sharpe handed a business card to the lawyer. "My cell number is on it. You can call her at that number." He turned for the door, gesturing for Sydney. "Come on. We have a plane to catch."

He acted like he didn't know—or didn't care—that she was upset, like she didn't have the right because she'd brought it on herself. A kernel of bitter anger took root in her chest, kindling and spreading through her body.

"Hey." She grabbed his arm, trying to ignore the jolt of awareness that sang through her at the feel of hard muscle beneath his suit jacket. But the sensation was so strong, so unexpected, that she fumbled for a second when he turned back and looked at her.

"What?"

Are you completely insensitive? she wanted to shout. What had happened to the guy on the boat? She wanted that Sharpe back, the one who'd held her, comforted her.

But she didn't ask those things, because what was the point? It wasn't his job to comfort her—it was his job to catch Tiberius, and he'd already made it clear that he didn't give a damn about her agenda or her feelings.

And maybe that was for the best, she realized, sucking in a breath. She had a feeling the sizzle she'd just felt wasn't one-sided, and that could complicate things. She couldn't become involved with him—getting involved would only serve to derail her from the important things.

She'd learned that lesson all too well before. It was her affair with Dr. Let's-share-ideas-so-I-can-steal-yours Richard Eckhart that'd led to the loss of her university position and gotten her set on this path in the first place.

So instead of asking for comfort, she said, "Why aren't you arguing about whether or not I should be at the scene?"

Sharpe looked down at her hand on his arm, then back up, so he was staring into her eyes when he said, "Because I never fight a battle I don't think I can win, Ms. Westlake. You might want to keep that in mind."

A thousand retorts jammed her brain, a thousand reasons why she should back off, back away and sit down with her lawyer while the FBI mobilized its forces to find Celeste. Instead of giving voice to any of that, though, she said simply, "Call me Sydney."

"Okay." But he didn't offer the same in return. Instead, he gestured to the door and the world beyond, which she hadn't seen in nearly a year. "Let's go."

She went.

Chapter Four

The flight from Boston to D.C. was a short hop, but even so, John could feel the awful tension in Sydney increasing by the minute.

He could only imagine what was going on inside her head—the guilt, the fear, the shame, the hope. He could only imagine it because he didn't have a sibling, didn't have a strong relationship with his parents…didn't really have anyone he truly loved, at least on the level other people seemed to feel the emotion. Iceman, indeed.

He had friends and coworkers, and that was plenty of attachments for him. However, that didn't mean he was unaware of the lengths other people would go to protect the ones they loved, and the agonies they suffered when those people were hurt, missing…or dead.

Sydney might have chosen her employer unwisely, and she might've let herself be pressured into doing unthinkable things with her scientific knowledge, but that didn't mean she wasn't grieving for her sister.

She sat beside him on the plane, still wearing the borrowed sweats. She had her head tipped back against the seat and her eyes closed as though she'd fallen asleep, but the tension written on her face and in the lines of her hands, which were gripped tightly together in her lap, warned that she wasn't sleeping. Maybe she was thinking of what she should've said or done differently, or maybe she was remembering happier times with her sister.

"Do you think she's dead?" she said, surprising him with the first words she'd uttered since they'd boarded.

"No."

She opened one eye and looked over at him. "I'd ask if you were just saying that to make me feel better, but I have a feeling that's not your thing."

"Good guess. I don't say things I don't mean, and I don't like repeating myself."

She closed her eyes again, and her face looked a little more relaxed than it had moments before. "You think Tiberius will keep her alive because if she's dead, he won't have anything else to threaten me with."

Except your own life, John thought. But she'd already committed to that risk when she escaped from the island. "That's the theory," he agreed.

"Which means that I should expect a ransom demand. The password in exchange for her life."

"There hadn't been any contact by the time the plane took off, and the locals were still searching the property and the nearby houses. She might've gotten away." He'd already passed on that update, but repeated the info because he thought it might help her to hear it again.

The realization brought him up short. He'd not only repeated himself, which he almost never did, but he'd also done it for no other reason than to make Sydney feel better. The very fact had faint warning buzzers going off in the back of his brain.

Keep it simple, he reminded himself. *Keep it in perspective.*

"It's unlikely she escaped," she said, her matter-of-factness ruined by the hitch in her voice. "It's hard for her to get around these days, even in the wheelchair."

He heard the hollow ring of guilt, and wondered how much of it was from the immediate situation, and how much was from the fact that the disease had apparently struck one twin and left the other untouched. He imagined there could be a large burden there, and wondered what it might motivate a person to do…like sign on with a killer.

And perhaps worse?

He stared at her in repose, trying to gauge what was happening here. His gut told him she'd gone into the job with good intentions. The question was how far would she be willing to go now to reach her goal.

"I never meant for any of this to happen," she said without opening her eyes. "Please believe that, if you believe nothing else about me."

Because he never said anything he didn't mean, he didn't respond to her statement. Instead he said, "Tell me more about the weapon."

A faint smile touched her lips and then fled to a frown, as though she was proud of the work, even as she hated what it had become. But when she spoke it was to ask him, "How much do you know about DNA fingerprinting?"

He'd done a quick info dump while she'd been

speaking with her lawyer. "I know the standard finger-print focuses on twenty places where the human DNA sequence varies in length from one person to the next. Each segment by itself might be the same length in two different people, but it's statistically impossible—or close enough for government work—for two people to be the same at every one of those segments by random chance. That's why they use twenty markers, to increase the statistical power of the analysis to the 'well beyond a shadow of a doubt' point."

She nodded, eyes still closed. "That's all true, but do you know why those segments vary in length?"

"Something about repeated letters." He'd skimmed over the techno-babble, figuring he'd get back to the nitty-gritty if he needed it.

"Not letters," she corrected, "dinucleotide repeats. The letters stand for the four nucleotides that make up the DNA molecule: A, C, T and G. They can be combined in all different orders for hundreds or even thousands of bases, and the cellular machinery reads them like a blueprint." She paused. "Anyway, the segments of DNA used for fingerprinting are essen-tially stretches of junk DNA—that means they're not used to encode a protein—made up of the nucleotides C and A, repeated over and over again. They're differ-ent lengths in different people because the repeats let the cellular machinery slip during DNA replication, mean-ing that a 'CA' unit might be added or deleted. As people have evolved over time, the repeats change in length."

John more or less got that, but not how it related to her sister. "If the fingerprints are taken from junk DNA, how does a technology aimed at Singer's syndrome morph into an antifingerprinting weapon?"

"Because there are other types of repeats. In particular, some coding genes have trinucleotide repeats, like the triplet CAG over and over again, for example. When these repeats slip and get bigger, the malfunctioning proteins translated from these genes can cause serious problems, like Huntington's disease."

"And Singer's syndrome," he finished for her.

"And Singer's," she repeated sadly.

"Your parents didn't know they carried the disease?"

"They died in a car crash when we were very young." Her voice was soft and sad. "And no, they didn't know. Repeat diseases like Singer's can lurk in what's called a 'premutation' form where the repeat is longer than normal, but not long enough to cause the disease. When the sperm or egg that became Celeste was forming, the repeat expanded further, meaning that she got the disease." She glanced at him from beneath lowered lids. "We're nonidentical twins. If we'd been identical, I'd probably be sick, too, depending on when the slip occurred."

"Do you blame yourself?" he asked, surprising himself with the question.

"That would be silly." They both knew that wasn't really an answer. "Besides, that's not the point, is it? The point is that Celeste does have it and I do feel guilty on some level. I also love my sister and want her alive and able to live her life to the fullest, so I went into Singer's research. Then my funding dried up…." She paused. He had a feeling there was more to that story than she was letting on, but before he could ask, she continued, "Tiberius made me an offer I couldn't refuse, and I convinced myself it was okay to let him use me as a legitimate front, as long as my work was going to help people."

"Only it wasn't."

"Exactly." She exhaled. "After about five months, once I'd designed the vector capable of suppressing the cell's ability to transcribe the expanded region and tricking it into making a normal protein instead, Tiberius gave me twenty new repeats he wanted me to work on in parallel. The moment I saw they were dinucleotide repeats, I knew what he was actually after."

John sent her a sharp look. "Just like that?"

She shifted uncomfortably and turned to look out the window, where the sky was starting to lighten with dawn. "Not exactly. I'd mentioned once or twice in passing that I thought repeat recognition technology could be used to block DNA fingerprinting."

He could tell from her body language she wasn't talking about a passing conversation among colleagues. "Let me guess. Research conference?"

She winced. "Worse. A review article."

He just shook his head. "Great." Now that the thought was out there, Tiberius probably wasn't the only one trying to develop the technology. Even once they took him down, they'd need some serious damage control, and probably a backup plan for CODIS.

"I'm sorry," she said softly.

He said nothing, because right at that moment he didn't have anything nice to say.

WHEN THEY REACHED D.C., one of the newer field agents was waiting to lead them to a big black SUV of the type most field offices were buying these days. The younger agent slapped a bubble light on the roof of the vehicle, and that, combined with a few strategic horn blips, was enough to get them through the city traffic and over to Glen Hills, Maryland, in under an hour.

Still mulling over what he'd learned from Sydney on the plane, John checked his messages and called for an update while they were en route.

He got his team's forensics expert, Drew Dietz. "There's practically nothing for forensics to work with," Drew reported. "And most of what we do have is probably going to trace back to the victims. Whoever was in here was good."

"Probably, but we're better," John said. "Keep at it." He hung up, and when Sydney looked over in inquiry, he shook his head. "Nothing yet."

She looked fragile and lost, sitting huddled against the far door with what felt like a mile between them, and for a second he was tempted to tell her everything was going to be okay.

But he didn't.

It was almost full light out when they pulled up in front of a stately old Victorian that easily dated back to the late 1800s but looked like it had been carefully updated in the years since, with modernizations that had maintained the historical charm. The shingles were painted some pale color he couldn't distinguish in the false light of dawn, the shutters and trim were accented in a darker hue and the grounds were landscaped neatly, if simply.

It might've looked like something out of a magazine, except for the police cruisers and black SUVs parked in the driveway and on the street in front of the house, in the typical hurried scatter that John knew indicated that violence had been done inside.

"Nice house." John decided he should just expect the unexpected when it came to Sydney Westlake. He would've pegged her for an ultramodern, superefficient condo. Instead, she lived in a painted lady.

"Before she got sick, Celeste wrote some seriously groundbreaking security programs. They pretty much paid for this place," Sydney said, answering his unspoken question. "The technology has moved on, though, and the residuals started drying up a couple of years ago. That was why—" She broke off, then correcting herself said, "That was partly why I took the job with Tiberius. We needed the money to keep this place up. I couldn't ask her to move, though. She's so happy here."

What about you? John wanted to ask, but didn't. Instead he said, "You ready to go in now, or would you rather wait until they've removed the bodies?"

She shuddered, but visibly collected herself and reached for the door handle. "Let's go. Maybe I'll see something that'll help us find Celeste."

As he followed her to the front door, John thought that was highly doubtful, given that she hadn't been in the house for a year, but he also knew she needed to go inside, needed to prove to herself that her sister was gone. He'd seen it before with victims' families, and would no doubt see it a thousand times more over the next couple of decades, because he was in this for life.

Major crimes—and the apprehension of major criminals—were in his blood. He hadn't gotten it from his globe-trotting musician parents, who lived for the next concert, the next party, and freely admitted they never should have reproduced. No, he'd gotten the cop gene from the uncle and great-uncle he'd visited during the short gaps between boarding school and sleep-away camp. Both of the older men had lived and died on the job, one as a cop, one as a Fed, neither married to anything but police work.

John figured he'd learned most of what he needed to know from them, including the dangers of becoming too friendly with witnesses, victims or snitches.

We're cops, not social workers, his great-uncle used to say. *Friendship doesn't change the evidence, but it can sure as hell change your perception of it. Better to leave affection out of things.*

Now, as he watched Sydney hesitate before pushing open the front door, the cynical part of John hoped she'd break down and tell him everything without waiting for execution of the immunity deal, and without withholding the parts she thought might help her if things went south. Another, deeply buried part of him—the part his great-uncle would've warned against—wished he could shield her from walking through her front door and seeing a handprint-size smear of blood on the lowest tread of the center stairwell, right beside the mechanical track her sister must've used to move her wheelchair from one floor to the next.

But he didn't shield her and he didn't stop her, and because he knew he wouldn't be able to talk her out of walking through to the kitchen, where the aide's body still lay where it had fallen, he didn't try to prevent her from heading to the scene of the crime. He walked beside her instead.

When she reached the threshold separating the kitchen and dining room, she stopped and swayed a little, but didn't back away, and John dropped the hand he'd instinctively raised to catch her if she fell.

The aide, a dark-haired twentysomething identified as Danielle Jones, lay on the tiled floor, sprawled where she'd fallen. She had two dime-size holes in her forehead, one centered, one off-center to the right and higher than the first. Both had leaked thin blood trails to the floor, where the droplets had fallen into the larger stain that spread from the exit wounds at the back of the victim's skull.

Two taps, John thought. *Professional.* According to Drew, it'd been the same with the other victim, the aide's boyfriend, Jay Alphonse. His body was in the garage, as though he'd been nailed on his way out.

There had been no passion to the kills. They had been pure practicality, a means to dispose of obstacles. Typical of Tiberius and his ilk.

Sydney sucked in a breath that sounded like a sob, and turned to him. "Where is my sister?"

He didn't answer because he'd already told her that her sister wasn't in the house, and telling her again was pointless.

Her eyes filled with tears. "She's really gone, isn't she?"

"I'm sorry," he said.

Her face crumpled and she seemed to collapse in on herself, her hands coming up to cover her face, her shoulders folding inward and shaking with silent sobs.

When her knees buckled and she headed for the floor, he reached out and caught her.

One piece of his brain said he was simply making sure she didn't mess up the scene, but in reality the move was pure instinct, just as it was instinct that had him folding her into his arms and holding her tight as she wept.

Just then, Drew strode in through the back. He stalled hard and his eyebrows hit his hairline when he saw his boss holding a sobbing woman in his arms.

Feeling a low burn in his gut, John snapped, "Anything new?"

"No— Ah, no. Sorry." Drew gestured with the film camera he used to photograph scenes. "I was just getting started with the pictures."

"Do it."

Drew bolted and John stared over the top of Sydney's head as she burrowed against him and sobbed into his chest. This was a good thing, he told himself. It was all about expediency. He'd wanted her to break so he could get the information he needed. None of this had anything to do with the feel of her in his arms, or the way she seemed to fit naturally against him, all soft curves and woman, urging his body to soften in some places, harden in others.

Drew stuck his head back through the door and made a point of not staring at them. "I had another look at—"

The phone rang, interrupting. John and Drew turned

toward the cordless unit, which sat alone at the center of the butcher-block island.

Sydney stiffened in his arms, as though suddenly realizing who she was clinging to, and maybe even wondering how that had come to be.

She pulled away, took a couple of steps into the kitchen and then looked at him for permission.

At Drew's signal that the handset had been processed, and Grace and Jimmy Oliverra had the trace and tape setups jacked into the phone line from the other room, John nodded. "Go ahead. Answer it."

She picked up the handset and hit the button to connect. "Hello?"

In the moment of silence that followed, John wished he had one of the headsets Grace and Jimmy were using to listen in. Seconds later, Sydney's whole body stiffened and she hissed a breath through her teeth before she shrieked, "You bastard. Where is she? Where is my sister? *What have you done with her?*"

John didn't need to wonder anymore; he knew. Tiberius was on the line, looking to make a deal of his own.

Chapter Five

"She's fine…for now." Tiberius's voice seemed to slither down the phone line, hissing into Sydney's ear where it curled, waiting to strike as he continued. "She'll stay that way, too, as long as you cooperate."

She didn't bother asking what he wanted. "Before I give you the password, I'm going to need some assurance that she's alive."

In her peripheral vision, she saw John surge forward a step and then stop himself, his expression dark and accusatory. He caught her eye and shook his head, mouthing, *Don't tell him the password*.

She frowned back at him. What did he think, she was stupid? If she gave up the password over the phone she'd never see her sister again.

"You're in no position to be making demands," Tiberius said, the slither turning cold and chilling her blood in her veins. "The password. Now."

Wrapping her free arm around herself and hugging the borrowed sweatshirt tight around her body, she turned away from the bloodstained kitchen and wandered out into the hall with the cordless phone pressed to her ear. She was aware that Sharpe followed, his steps nearly silent, making her feel stalked and protected at the same time.

Ignoring him, she moved into the sitting room, which contained a small television and three walls worth of books. Interspersed amongst the paperbacks and research books were photographs of her and Celeste, over and over, just the two of them, spanning from earliest childhood to the previous year, as they'd lived their lives out together.

Tears misted Sydney's vision, forcing her to pinch the bridge of her nose to hold them back.

"I'm not giving you the password now," she said with a faint quiver in her voice from nerves at what she was about to propose. "And I'm not doing it over the phone. It has to be in person. I'll meet you—"

She broke off as her eyes locked on one photo, a special picture that showed Celeste and her kayaking in Puget Sound. It had been the summer before Celeste had gotten sick. They'd had plenty of money from the sale of her computer programs, and Sydney's new university job hadn't started until fall, so they'd worked their way across the country. It'd been the best summer Sydney could remember.

And the picture was upside down.

"Oh, hell."

"Excuse me?" Tiberius said, in a tone that indicated she'd managed to surprise the master of surprises.

"I'm not trading the password for a bluff, Tiberius. Sorry. You lose this round."

When she clicked the phone off, hanging up on the

criminal mastermind, the two agents manning the phone tap gaped and squawked, and fiddled with their equipment in an effort to get the call back.

Sharpe didn't move, though. He watched her, face expressionless, as she dropped the phone and hurried to the bookcase.

Heart pounding, she grabbed the framed picture and twisted it a hundred-eighty degrees on the hidden rod that went from the back of the old frame, through the wall and into a mechanism that the contractors she'd used for the renovations thought might date back to Prohibition. Metal grated against metal and a section of wall swung inward on heavy, hand-forged hinges, revealing a dark corridor that traveled inward a few feet and took an immediate ninety-degree turn. The small bolt hole in front of them was empty. Beyond the turn, no light penetrated farther into the hidden tunnel.

But there were two parallel lines in the dust, exactly the width apart of a wheelchair's wheels.

Celeste. Afraid to say her sister's name in case she'd been wrong, in case Tiberius wasn't bluffing after all and he'd somehow gotten her after she'd made it to the bolt hole, Sydney surged forward toward the passageway.

An iron-strong hand gripped her arm, pulling her back.

"I go first," Sharpe said, and did just that, heading into the passageway with his weapon drawn. Seconds later she heard him hiss a curse.

Ignoring the others, she plunged into the darkness after him.

Two steps in, she slammed into him where he'd stopped dead. Though she'd been going full tilt, he weathered the impact easily, holding out an arm to keep her from falling. "Easy there."

"Celeste?" she whispered, clinging to his arm for reassurance, though she knew damn well he was the last person she should be leaning on.

"Yes," he said. "And yes, she's alive. She's unconscious, but her pulse is steady and her breathing seems okay. The chair seems to be wedged or something. If you back up a little, I think I can get it free."

Sydney pretty much stopped processing his words after *Yes, she's alive.* Relief shivered through her, followed by a wash of nausea and guilt. This was her fault, all of it. If she hadn't taken that job—

Stop, she told herself. Stop there. What was done was done. She couldn't go back and undo it, so she was going to have to find a way to make the best while moving forward. She was going to have to find a way to fix what she'd messed up so badly.

Still, she whispered, "Thank you." She wasn't sure whether she meant it for the man ahead of her in the secret passageway or for some celestial being looking down on her from up above, but she knew one thing for sure: she'd gotten lucky with Celeste.

The aide and her boyfriend, however, hadn't been lucky at all. Their blood would remain on Sydney's hands.

She heard the catch of metal on leather as Sharpe holstered his weapon and tried to work the heavy, mechanized chair free and drag it out into the main room.

"You've got to put the transmission in Neutral," she said, stepping forward and reaching past him to work the controls in the darkness.

In the close quarters, she had to squeeze tightly against him to reach the mechanism. They wound up pressed together, with her shoulder and arm against his torso and her leg touching his from hip to ankle. It was impossible not to notice that they lined up perfectly in all the right spots, and that he was warm and strong and incredibly male.

It might've been partly relief at finding Celeste, might've been the sensation of finally being home after so long, but the giddy rush of excitement seemed to come, not from the circumstances, but from the man. But when she found herself wanting to lean into him and stay there, she made herself pull away instead.

"There." Her voice came out high and breathy, and she forced it level before continuing, "You should be able to move it now."

She backed out of the passageway as Sharpe wheeled Celeste out of the darkness and into the light.

As he did so, her eyelids flickered.

"We'll want the paramedics in here, Grace," he said quietly to the short, dark-haired woman who'd been one of the two agents manning the phone trace.

Grace nodded and headed outside, but Sydney couldn't wait. She knelt down beside Celeste's chair and took one of her sister's cool hands, rubbing it between her own. "Celeste, hon? You in there? Knock, knock?"

It was their sad little inside joke, because Celeste was always "in there." Sometimes, though, she couldn't get out past the shell of her own body.

Singer's syndrome was a progressive debilitating neuropathy, which as far as Sydney could tell was a fancy way of saying that Celeste's mind was sharp as ever but her body was giving out on her day by day, as plaques of a faulty neural protein—the one containing the expanded trinucleotide repeat—built up along her nerve fibers. The more it accumulated, the harder it was for Celeste's brain to get neural impulses to her extremities.

She could still hold a pen on her good days. On the bad days, she had to rely on her chair, which could be operated by a press-and-puff joystick affixed at mouth-level.

At least that had been the situation when Sydney left. Now, as Celeste's eyelids fluttered open and her sky-blue eyes locked on her sister, Sydney wondered whether she'd deteriorated even further and faster than they'd both feared she would. Her hand remained cool and lax in Sydney's, and she didn't react right away, just sat there, eyes dreamy.

Then, as if she'd bumped up against a live wire, Celeste gasped, yanked upright in her chair and grabbed onto Sydney's hand.

Yet still, she didn't speak.

"Thank God." Sydney exhaled a long, relieved breath and leaned in to gather her sister close. "I was so worried." The words were completely inadequate, but what else could she say just then?

"Danielle and Jay are dead, aren't they?" Celeste whispered, voice trembling.

"Yes, they are. Thank God you made it into the hidey-hole."

"I just…" Celeste's eyes filled. "Your last e-mail warned me to watch out, that something bad might happen."

Sharpe cleared his throat.

"Celeste, honey," Sydney said. "This is Agent Sharpe of the FBI. He needs to ask you some questions."

"Did you see the killer?" he asked quietly. Behind him, several other agents and police officers were hard at work on the crime scene.

Celeste shook her head. "No. I'm sorry."

"Don't be sorry," Sydney responded immediately. "If he'd seen you…" She trailed off and swallowed hard, then pressed her cheek against Celeste's and repeated in a whisper, "Don't be sorry. Ever."

Celeste leaned into the embrace, but her voice was stronger and a little reproving when she said, "I'm not going to say I told you so."

"Then I'll say it," Sydney replied. "You told me so."

Celeste had wanted her to turn down the job on Rocky Cliff Island. They had argued back and forth for nearly a week before Sydney left, and the parting had been more bitter than sweet.

The homecoming was proving far worse.

Grace stuck her head around the corner to report, "The paramedics are here."

Celeste submitted to a quick vitals check, then waved them off. "I'm as fine as I get." She looked at Sharpe. "Besides, I have a feeling your fed here wants to ask me some questions."

"He's not my fed," Sydney said, and damned the flush that touched her cheeks.

Sharpe didn't crouch down to talk to Celeste, which gained him points in Sydney's eyes. Instead, he dropped into a nearby chair so he and Celeste were eye level with each other before he said, "Do you feel up to answering a few questions?"

Celeste glanced at Sydney and raised an eyebrow in a look of, *How much should I tell him?*

"He's okay," Sydney said. "Tell him everything you remember about what just happened."

In other words, *Don't say anything about Rocky Cliff Island or the e-mailed computer programs.*

Sharpe glanced at Sydney and scowled faintly. "I guess that will have to do. For now." Then he turned to Celeste. "Please backtrack as far as you're willing to go, and walk me through last night and early this morning. Tell me whatever you remember about the attacks. I'm recording this, okay?" He held up a PDA, and at her nod, keyed it to record.

She described her normal bedtime routine, then waking up and hearing strange noises, and thinking that Danielle's boyfriend was trying to sneak out before she woke up again. "I heard what sounded like silenced gunshots, you know, like they sound on TV," Celeste said. "I tried my cell phone but it wasn't working, like it was jammed or something. Right about then I figured out it was a break-in, and I got myself strapped into my wheels." She tried to pat the armrest and managed little more than a feeble flip of her hand.

That told Sydney that she was getting low on energy. She touched her sister's hand. "You should rest."

"I'm fine," Celeste snapped.

Trying not to feel the sting of a reunion that wasn't anything like she imagined, Sydney pulled her hand back and said softly, "I'm just trying to help."

"So am I." Celeste turned back to Sharpe and continued, "I wheeled myself out into the hall and used the stair lift to get downstairs. Thank God they didn't hear me."

"They?" He hadn't moved, but Sydney sensed his attention shift, focusing more precisely. "Are you sure there was more than one?"

"Positive. I saw—" Celeste broke off and swallowed. "I saw them leaning over something in the kitchen. I saw blood…and I went the other way."

Sydney could see her sister's frustration growing, her anger at a body that let her down over and over. And though Sydney knew it wasn't her fault she was healthy and her sister was ill, guilt stung anyway.

When a tear trickled down Celeste's cheek, Sydney announced, "That's it. We're done for now."

"No, we're not," Celeste snapped. "Look, Syd, I know you're trying to help, but you're just getting in the poor guy's way." Sharpe looked mildly surprised to be called a poor guy, but kept his mouth shut as Celeste continued, "Either stop fussing and let me finish, or go sit upstairs or something."

"You're tired," Sydney said softly. "You know how you get cranky when your energy runs low."

Celeste narrowed her eyes. "Yeah, and I get cranky when you treat me like a toddler, too. I'm wheelchairbound, not a vegetable. Give me some credit for knowing when to say when." As Sydney's mouth dropped open, she smiled a little. "You've been gone nearly a year, Syd. Surprise." She turned back to Sharpe. "I know for sure there were at least two of them, but I only saw them from the back, and nothing really stood out. Dark clothes, dark caps, medium builds. One was shorter than the other. The one—" She broke off and swallowed hard. "The one with the gun was wearing gloves. I didn't see the other guy's hands. It was all so quick. When I realized what they'd done, all I could think to do was hide in the secret passageway. I knew they'd hear me if I tried to go out the front, and it was so late…" She trailed off. "I just…hid."

"Best thing you could've done," Sharpe said, without on ounce of coddling or softness in his voice. "The only way for you to help is to help us catch them, and you've got to be alive to do that."

Sydney knew that his blunt words probably meant more to her sister than a hundred reassurances from her.

Celeste sniffed, nodded and finished, "I'd just gotten the door shut behind me—there's another lever on the inside that locks the mechanism—when I heard footsteps going upstairs, then some banging, like they were looking for me. I just…stayed there. I heard the front door slam, like, five minutes later, but I was too scared to move. After a while, I must have dozed off."

Browned out was more like it, Sydney thought, but she didn't want Celeste to feel like she was hovering.

Over the past eleven months she'd missed her sister like crazy. They'd never been apart for more than a few weeks at a time before, and she'd pictured their reunion like one big party, had figured that after she was home everything would go back to normal.

But that was before she figured out what Tiberius really wanted from her, and how far he was willing to go to get it.

"What happens now?" Celeste asked.

"There's an agent on his way named Hugo Thorn-ridge," Sharpe said. "He's gong to take care of you."

Sydney drew a breath to speak, but Celeste silenced her with a look before saying, "Take care of me how, exactly?"

"He's a registered nurse with medic training." The agent paused. "He's also a sniper-trained sharpshooter, has a black belt in one of the martial arts and throws a hell of a punch in a bar fight." A touch of a smile suggested there was a story there. "He'll help you monitor your health, and he'll be in charge of your safety."

"You're putting me in witness protection," Celeste said. It wasn't a question.

He shook his head. "Not exactly. WITSEC is a formal program, complete with paperwork and processing. We don't have time for that, and frankly I'm not sure it's as secure as it needs to be when dealing with someone like Tiberius. You and Hugo are going underground. He'll check in with me regularly, and leave updates on your position when he deems prudent, but other than that, you two will be totally off the grid."

Sydney made a sad, pained noise. Danielle and Jay were dead. Celeste was going to be running for her life. All because she'd gone to work for Tiberius.

"Hey, Syd." Celeste made a faint motion with her hand. "You didn't do this. Tiberius did."

Sydney stifled a sob and took Celeste's hand, pressing it to her cheek. But she didn't say anything, because they both knew the truth was that Tiberius hadn't been acting alone. She had played along with him for far too

long, and now she, her sister and the people around
them were paying the price for her mistakes.

So much for a joyous reunion, where she brought
back a cure for her sister and money for them both to
live on abroad, then phoned in an anonymous tip on
Tiberius and his island of horrors.

Instead, she'd returned home to two more innocent
victims and a sister she barely recognized.

While Celeste and Sharpe spoke briefly, Sydney
stared at her sister. She still looked the same. Her
straight, midbrown hair was bobbed at her shoulders and
her face was a slightly thinner rearrangement of
Sydney's own features, with the exception of blue eyes
instead of brown. Her arms and legs were far too thin,
due to the wasting effects of the disease, and for the
most part the only motion came from her mouth and
eyes, with an occasional laborious hand gesture for
emphasis. There was nothing really stand-out different
about her.

She was the same. Yet she wasn't. She'd gotten herself out of bed and hidden, outsmarting a pair of trained
killers. And she'd snapped at Sydney not once but twice,
when before she would've agreed that yes, she was
tired. Yes, she should rest and not get overexcited.

Did I hold her back? Sydney wondered now. *Did I
make it too easy for her to be sick?*

"Sydney," Sharpe said, his voice sharp enough to
indicate he was repeating himself. "You with us?"

"Sorry." She shook her head, trying to clear it. But
how could she possibly clear everything that was inside
her skull at this point? It was all tangled up together in

one big messy knot: the joy of finding Celeste unharmed; the hurt of seeing that she was doing okay—if not better—on her own; the pain of two more people dying because of her… "It's all too much," she whispered.

It wasn't until Celeste squeezed her hand that she realized they were still sitting close together, that she finally had her sister by her side once again.

Then Celeste said, "Hugo's here. We need to say goodbye now."

"But—" Sydney stopped herself and bowed her head to hide the tears. "I know."

A big man appeared in the front doorway, filling it from one side to the other. He had short blond hair and pleasantly regular features, with a glint of humor in his light blue eyes. Wearing cargo pants held up by a web belt, combat boots and a khaki T-shirt stretched across his wide chest, he practically screamed ex-military, and instantly made Sydney feel better about Celeste going into hiding.

She looked up at him. "Please tell me that you're Hugo."

"My thoughts exactly," Celeste murmured from beside her, and Sydney stifled a grin, feeling a little lift beneath her heart at the realization that somehow, somewhere, she'd gotten back a part of the sister she remembered.

"That'd be me." He looked at Celeste and raised a golden eyebrow. "You ready to boogie?"

"Yes, please." Her face clouded. "I'd like to get out of here."

Sydney felt a pang at the realization that they'd probably never share their pretty little house again. Not only would she need to sell it to cover the legal bills she was no doubt racking up by the second, but she also couldn't imagine either of them wanting to live there after two people had died so horribly in the kitchen.

"Hey, sis." Celeste used her faltering strength to tug on her hand. "Take care of yourself."

"You, too." Sydney bent and hugged her sister, harder than she probably should have, but needing to prove to herself that they were both there, that they were both okay, for the moment at least.

Hugo had pulled a specially outfitted van up very close to the door, since the garage was roped off with crime scene tape. He draped a pair of Kevlar vests over Celeste for the short trip out in the open.

The precautions reassured Sydney. At the same time they made her want to throw up.

"Tell me she'll be okay," she said to the man she sensed standing directly behind her.

"Hugo's one of the best," Sharpe said. "If anyone can keep her off Tiberius's radar, he can."

She nodded. "Thank you."

He said nothing, though she didn't know if it was because he didn't want her thanks, or if his mind was already elsewhere, moving on to the next topic, the next fight.

She turned to him, battling the almost overwhelming compulsion to lean on him, just for a moment, and absorb some of the strength he seemed to wear like a second skin. "What happens now?"

He glanced down at her. "We're going to put you in a safe house under full guard. At that point I will

have fulfilled my part of the bargain by getting you
and your sister protected to the best of my ability.
Then it's going to be your turn." His voice went low,
but not in the slightest bit soft. "You're going to tell
us how to fight Tiberius and keep him from taking
down CODIS."

SEVERAL HUNDRED miles away, sitting in the elegant
kitchen of a renovated Vermont farmhouse that was
owned under the little-used alias Kyle Cross, Tiberius
slapped the phone shut with a bitter oath.

The thick-maned redhead sitting at the other end of
the long breakfast bar, still wearing one of the skin-tight
flight suits she favored when piloting Tiberius's
chopper, looked up from buffing a chip out of one of her
nails. "Problem, darling?"

"Nothing that can't be dealt with," he responded,
feeling a measure of calm at the knowledge of just how
true those words were. His guards might have let
Sydney Westlake escape from the island—and they'd be
punished for the lapse—and the contractors he'd hired
in Maryland might've screwed up the sister's capture,
ditto on the retribution, but that didn't mean he was
entirely without options.

He tapped the computer screen of his high-tech
phone, bringing up an encrypted list, and keyed in the
code required to translate the names, revealing a list of
key FBI personnel that he'd either found useful in the
past, or who had weaknesses he knew he could exploit.
A quick comparison between that list and the names
he'd gotten for John Sharpe's major crimes team,

followed by a brief phone call, and he had himself a new employee.

Sydney wasn't going to know what hit her.

Chapter Six

Sydney spent the next four days in a safe house outside D.C., downloading her brain into huge databases and modeling programs run by two of Sharpe's people— pretty, soft-spoken Grace Mears and quirky, geeky Jimmy Oliverra.

There was no sign of Sharpe. He didn't visit, didn't call. He might as well have taken Celeste away himself, because she hadn't heard a peep from either of them.

Telling herself he didn't owe her an accounting of his whereabouts, Sydney forced herself to focus on the laptop screen, which showed a satellite photo of Rocky Cliff Island. It was near dusk on day four, and she was losing her edge. She was sick of the safe house, sick of being cooped up, sick of going over the same information again and again, until it was all starting to blur together in her head.

She'd already told them everything she thought was relevant about the DNA vector, and the computer programs currently guarding it. Now they were working on constructing a virtual model of Rocky Cliff Island. At first the agents had been concerned that Tiberius might have left the island for good; none of the initial passes of the retasked satellite had shown evidence of him being in residence. But that didn't make any sense—there was no way for him to get the DNA sequence off the island without the password, short of moving each and every computer without disrupting the networked connections.

Sure enough, on the previous day his helicopter had touched down on the pad just uphill of the mansion, and word had come down from Sharpe—relayed through Jimmy, of course—that they were to model "every damn last beach plum on the godforsaken piece of rock" in case they needed to plan a raid.

Sydney was pretty sure that was close to verbatim, and she was more than a little horrified that she kept replaying the words in her mind, imagining the way they'd sound in his deep, resonant voice.

Forcing herself to focus on the job at hand, she pointed to a small white box on the extreme eastern point of the narrow, oblong island. "That's a guard shack, one of the big ones. It's got some sort of weapon on the top, hidden under a second, false roof." She glanced at the others and shrugged slightly. "Sorry, but I only saw it once on my way in. I'm not sure I can do much more with the details."

Jimmy broke off the low, tuneless whistling he maintained while working his machines. "Don't be sorry. Just do your best." That was pretty much Jimmy's attitude toward life, which made him a good match for type-A, intense Grace, who immediately began tapping away at her computer.

Within seconds, the screen in front of Sydney had the

guard shack labeled as such. Next, Grace tapped a few more keys and a new page popped up, showing schematic renderings of some seriously nasty-looking turret-type guns that looked like they could take out anything from an airplane to a medium-size boat. "Anything look familiar?" she asked.

Sydney closed her eyes, trying to remember what the weapon had looked like. "It was longer and...thinner at the end, I think." They went through a few iterations before she nodded. "That's as close as I can get."

"We'll take it." Jimmy spun the image of the island on-screen, focusing their view in on another structure. "How about this one?"

Grace's e-mail program gave a *ping* signaling incoming mail. Sydney automatically glanced at the screen. She saw *J.Sharpe* in boldface.

Grace spun the screen away from her before opening the message. She shot Sydney an uncomfortable sidelong look. "Sorry."

"You're just following orders," Sydney said softly, "It's not your fault he doesn't trust me. It's mine." What she didn't say was how much his mistrust bothered her, how much she wished things had started off differently between them.

She kept trying to tell herself it was the isolation of the safe house that had her hyperfocused on Sharpe, but that didn't play because she'd been just as isolated—if not more so—in the lab on Rocky Cliff Island, and she hadn't spent her time fantasizing about any of her guards, or thinking about her ex, Richard, or hell, imagining herself with Gabriel Byrne or one of the dark-haired hunks she usually gravitated toward in the movies.

No, she had Special Agent John Sharpe on the brain. Special Agent John Sharpe, who hadn't spoken to her in four days and twelve hours, and who, as far as she could tell, wanted nothing more from her than information.

"He doesn't trust anybody," Grace corrected. "That's why he's so good at his job."

"I'm betting it doesn't make him much of a hit in the social department," Sydney observed. She pushed back her chair at the kitchen table they were using as a workspace, and crossed the tiled floor to open the refrigerator and peer inside, just in case something interesting had magically appeared in there since the last time she'd checked. Which had been, oh, fifteen minutes or so earlier.

"Why do you ask?" Grace's look was sly.

"Just looking for a weak spot." Sydney sighed and shut the fridge before hiking herself up onto the kitchen counter. She was wearing jeans and a clingy red sweater she'd thought would cheer her up when she'd gotten dressed that morning. Her feet were laced into a pair of sneakers, even though it was doubtful she'd be going anywhere.

The shoes were a house rule, though: be ready to run, in case something bad happens.

"Sharpe doesn't have any weak spots," Grace said. "A few dents, maybe, but no gaps in the armor."

Don't ask, Sydney told herself, but did it anyway. "Dents?"

That earned her a long look, but Grace answered, "There was a woman a few years back. A witness. It ended badly."

"Ahem." Jimmy tapped the computer screen. "Not to interrupt, but…"

"I saw men coming and going from that one once, carrying things," Sydney said. "Storeroom, maybe?"

"Can you define 'things'?"

"Not really. I was pretty far away." Sydney tried to concentrate, but what she really wanted to do was ask about Sharpe's ex. What sort of witness had she been? What exactly did "end badly" mean? Had it been a simple breakup that'd turned awkward, or had it been a double cross, like she'd had with Richard? Or worse, had it been a more final end, like *bang dead?*

"We need a different satellite," Jimmy groused, flipping through the views of the island. "I want thermals, high-def, that sort of thing."

"Can't do it," Grace responded. "No tasking other satellites until further notice—Sharpe wants to keep all the info gathering in-house. His paranoia has kicked in. He's got it in his head that Tiberius might be working with someone on the inside."

That froze Sydney. "Why does he think that?" *And does it mean I'm not safe here anymore? Does it mean Tiberius knows where Celeste is?*

"Because he's a paranoid bastard," a new voice said from the doorway.

Sydney gasped and spun, her heart freezing in her chest, then starting up again—entirely too fast—when she saw Sharpe standing there with his arms folded over his chest and his long, lean body propped up against the doorframe.

He was wearing a dark gray suit and pale gray shirt, with a brightly patterned tie shoved in his breast pocket as though he'd worn it for a meeting and yanked it off immediately after. His eyes were dark, his expression unreadable, and the combined effect made the whole package seriously drool worthy.

A quiver took up residence in Sydney's stomach. Damn it. She'd spent the past four days trying not to think about him—and failing miserably. Yet even at that, she'd forgotten how gorgeous he actually was.

Without meaning to, she took a step back, so she was even with Grace's chair. Glancing down at the computer specialist, Sydney realized the woman hadn't moved, hadn't reacted to the surprise.

Ergo, she hadn't been surprised.

"You could've warned me he was here," Sydney muttered under her breath.

"Could've," Grace agreed, "but I do so hate being predictable."

She casually tilted the computer so Sydney could read the brief e-mail giving his ETA at the safe house. The note gave no hint why he was there, nor did the closed expression on his strong, elegant face give any insight into his thoughts.

Suddenly, though, Sydney had the strongest feeling that he hadn't come to speak with his teammates. He'd come for her.

"Is something wrong?" she took a step toward him. "Celeste?"

"Hugo hasn't missed a check-in," he said. It wasn't the same thing as "they're fine" but she knew it was probably the best she was going to get out of him.

Where have you been? she wanted to ask. *Have you been busy? Were you avoiding me?* But she kept those questions to herself, because he didn't owe her comfort, or an explanation. So instead she asked, "Why are you here?"

His eyes fixed on her and darkened, and there was a click of connection. Heat flared in her center, urging her to cross the short distance between them and touch the strong line of his jaw, tempting her to dig her fingers into his hair and hang on for the ride.

And from the heat that flared in his eyes when he looked at her, she wasn't the only one feeling the urge.

"Grace said you were getting stir-crazy." His voice had gone slightly rough, and the sound thrilled along her nerve endings like a caress. "She thought it'd do you some good to get out of here."

"I'd kill to," she said without thinking, then winced. "Figuratively, I mean. Sorry, I'm still not used to being around people who don't necessarily consider that a figure of speech."

"Noted." Sharpe unfolded himself from the doorway and gestured toward the front door of the heavily guarded safe house. "You want to go or not?"

Sydney hung back, sudden nerves gathering alongside the heat of excitement in her belly. "Is it safe?"

"You'll be wearing a vest and the location we're going to is secure." Again, not an absolute promise of safety. Just the facts, ma'am.

"Are you—" She broke off and swallowed hard. "Is this a plan to draw out the men who killed Danielle and Jay?"

"Would that bother you?"

"Not if I knew I was being used as bait."

He gave her a long, assessing look. She wasn't sure if he was trying to decide whether she was telling the truth, or if she'd surprised him. After a moment he said, "We already have the two men who broke in to your house."

"You captured them?" If that was where he'd been, he was entirely forgiven.

But he shook his head. "We found them…or rather what was left of them when Tiberius was through." He paused. "The prints of one of the men match the partials from your kitchen—he must've been the one not wearing gloves. The other guy had traces of blood on one of his shoes. We're running the DNA now, but I'd be surprised if it doesn't match one or both of the victims." He didn't say where they'd been found or how they died and she didn't ask.

She didn't really think she wanted to know.

"That leaves us right back where we started," Sydney said, staring at her toes on a beat of sadness. Guilt tugged at the thought of the domino chain she'd helped initiate. Yes, Tiberius was ultimately responsible for the killings, but so much of the violence had been initiated by her actions.

"Not entirely. We know more than we did before," he countered. "And Tiberius is back on the island. I have a feeling things are going to break loose in the next few days, one way or the other."

Sydney shivered, not wanting to know what "the

other" might entail. "Can't you just, I don't know, blow up the island or something?"

His blue eyes glinted with a brief flash of amusement. "That's not exactly kosher in the due process department. At the moment, we don't even have enough to justify a raid on the mansion." He grimaced, his frustration evident. "That's according to our higher-ups, anyway. They want this done squeaky clean and by the books. He's slipped away too many times before. We're not taking that chance again. Besides—" now his expression turned sardonic "—I thought you wanted to protect your work. Isn't that why you froze the machines rather than blanking them completely?"

"That, and because I figured I'd need the leverage if he caught me," she answered honestly.

"You were going to trade the password for your freedom." It wasn't a question.

"Of course." Her voice went defensive. "I was going to send everything I had to the authorities the moment I thought Celeste and I were safely hidden."

"That plan has two major flaws," Sharpe pointed out. "One, you and your sister will never truly be safe from him until he's either dead or behind bars. And two, by the time you dropped the dime, he could've easily sold your bug. The damage would've already been done."

Something in his eyes alerted her. "You know what he plans to do with the virus."

He tipped his head. "We have a pretty good guess." But he didn't elaborate, emphasizing that he might be using her for information, but she wasn't really part of the team. Glancing at Grace and Jimmy, who had given up all pretense of working and were avidly watching the exchange, Sharpe said, "Speaking of which, don't you two have work to do?"

Jimmy grinned, unrepentant. "Yes, but this is way more entertaining."

Sharpe grimaced and waved in the direction of the front door, and the deepening night beyond. He said to Sydney, "Do you want to get out of here or not?"

Something in his body language warned her that it wasn't nearly that simple. "You're sure it's not a trap?"

"No. It's pizza under armed guard by yours truly. You in or out?" He said it like he didn't care which way she went, but there was a subtle challenge in his tone.

"I'm in," she said finally, wondering why it felt like she'd just agreed to more than pizza.

"Good. I'll get the Kevlar. Meet me by the front door." He turned on his heel and strode out, leaving Sydney staring at the empty doorway.

She shot a look at Grace. "Was that a little strange, or is it my imagination?"

Grace looked torn, as though she didn't want to talk about her team leader out of turn—especially with him potentially within earshot.

Jimmy had no such compunction, saying, "Yeah, this isn't his usual style." He paused and lifted one shoulder in a half shrug. "Thing is, you can trust Sharpe to say exactly what he means. If he says he's not using you as bait, then he's not using you as bait."

The statement implied he was very likely planning to use her for some other purpose she hadn't yet guessed at.

Since that lined up with Sydney's own gut check, she nodded. "Okay. I guess I'll see you guys later."

"I'm headed out." Jimmy stood and cracked his knuckles. "Hot date."

Grace rolled her eyes in a look of *yeah, right,* and said, "Don't worry. I'll be here, slaving away." She sketched a wave and bent back over her laptop keyboard.

Which left Sydney with one last question as she grabbed her jacket and headed for the front door: why pizza?

JOHN WAS ASKING himself a similar question forty minutes later as he turned off the highway and headed his car along the outskirts of the D.C. commuter belt, toward the restored farmhouse he called home in-between road assignments.

Why was he taking Sydney home with him? Why hadn't he just stuck her in witness protection along with her sister and forgotten about them both while he went on with the investigation?

And why, when he came down to it, had he added dinner to the mix?

He'd picked up the pizza on the way through town. The box sat on the backseat, steaming the interior of the car with the spicy smells of garlic and tomatoes, along with the greasy promise of melted cheese.

The food, along with his last-minute decision to drive his own wheels rather than a company car, made the scenario feel too much like a date. Worse was the fleeting thought of whether she'd like the place, and the hope that she wouldn't mind eating in the living room because the dining table was snowed in under a drift of psych magazines, gun journals, prison newsletters and just about anything else he could get his hands on that could give him new insight into the heads of major criminals like Tiberius.

And he was losing his mind.

He'd told himself to stay away from her. He'd even managed to follow through…for four whole days. Four days during which he'd done his job but been unable to get her out of his head. Four days of flipping open his phone intending to call her, then forcing himself to put the unit back in his pocket without dialing.

Everything she'd told them had checked out. She was who she said she was, and events prior to her leaving for the island had occurred pretty much as she'd reported. She'd lost her funding following an incident with her immediate boss that'd been clouded with enough academic double-speak to tell him they'd been lovers. The fact that the knowledge bothered him—the fact that he cared at all—was just one more warning buzzer amidst the sirens already sounding off inside his skull.

As he turned the car off the highway, he glanced over at Sydney, who'd stayed silent during the drive, lost in her own thoughts.

She stared out the window, and the passing streetlights highlighted the soft curve of her cheek and the elegant column of her neck above the bulk of the Kevlar vest. When he turned off the main road down the side street that would take them to his home, the streetlights gave way to darkness. The faint blue glow from the dashboard dials gave her profile a dreamy quality, one that made him think of bedrooms and fantasies, which should've had no place in his head.

He was willing to believe she wasn't working for Tiberius anymore. Her relationship with her sister was real, as were her initial motivations for taking the job on Rocky Cliff Island. The decision had been a poor one, but she'd learned her lessons the hard way. She was cooperating as best she could, trying to fix the mess she'd helped make.

But although she might not fall under the "suspect" category in his brain anymore, that only served to make her a witness. And he knew better than to mess with witnesses.

Which begged the question of what the hell he thought he was doing now. This was so stupid it was almost laughable, yet he'd been unable to stop himself from driving to the safe house, unable to stay away any longer.

He had, quite simply, needed to see her.

What was it about her that made him so crazy? He didn't know. Sure, she was pretty. A knockout, really, with those long runner's legs and perfectly proportioned body. And her hands—he'd never really thought about a woman's hands before, but he'd noticed hers. They were strong and capable-looking, yet tapered and feminine, and she had this way of lifting her fingertips to her face or brow as she spoke, making him want that feather-light touch on his own skin.

And that was the point, wasn't it? She'd drawn him in, wrapped him around those same fingers until, in that first crazy moment when he'd walked into the safe house and seen her for the first time in days, she could've had him with a single finger-crook.

Something had to give. Starting now. Tonight. He had to find a way to purge her from his system, a way to convince himself once and for all that he had to stay away from her, had to keep his hands to himself.

Either that or he had to have her.

Iceman, my ass, he thought, as he turned the car down the narrow, tree-lined driveway to their destination. He hated the loss of control, hated feeling as if he was spinning in unfamiliar directions, ready to snap at a touch. But at the same time, the edgy energy was tempting—dark and delicious, and so unlike his normal self that he wanted to give in, just once, and see what it felt like to be ruled by the heat.

It was full night, but the moon was out, showing the three-rail fence of the paddocks and glinting off the tin-roofed run-in sheds as he rolled the car up the dirt road to the house.

"Horses?" Sydney glanced at him. "That's pretty expensive camouflage for a safe house."

"It's not a safe house," he corrected. "And there aren't any horses at the moment. Just the sheds and paddocks."

Horses were in his long-range plans, though, along with a dog. He planned to fill the place with life when it was time for him to slow down…in twenty years or so, when he retired from the job.

He'd had a pony one summer, when camp plans had fallen through and he'd been packed off to his great-uncle's place. The neighbors had a pony their kids had long outgrown, and John's great-uncle, also named

John, had borrowed the creature for the summer on the theory that every kid should have a pony at least once in their lives.

The furry, stumpy creature of unknown ancestry had tossed the younger John in the dirt as often as it let him stay aboard, and it had bitten like a viper, but it'd been there every damn day, waiting for him to spend time with it, brushing and cleaning it, mucking its stall and hauling water and hay until his back had ached and his arms had quivered with the strain.

And he'd loved every minute of it. He'd loved the responsibility, and the knowledge that the pony would be there at the gate, every day, waiting for him. He hadn't had a pet in all the years since, but always figured he'd get back to it. Someday.

He parked in front of the house, which was one of his few prides outside the job. Built in the late 1700s, it'd undergone a series of expensive—and often misguided—renovations over the years before he found it through a friend of a friend, who'd seen it as a good investment and nothing more. When John bought the place, it'd been covered in vinyl siding and faux Victorian trim, and had been inexplicably painted a weird blue-green.

Slowly, layer-by-layer, he was pulling back the changes and unearthing the charm beneath.

"Whose place is this?" Sydney asked as she climbed out of the car.

John climbed out of his side and crossed to her, but he didn't feel the need to rush her inside, out of the open. They hadn't been followed, and there was no way

Tiberius could connect him to the farm. He'd made sure of that when he bought the place, needing to know he had a refuge if and when it became necessary.

"It's mine," he answered, using the remote unit on his key ring to disarm the perimeter alarms, which had started counting down from sixty seconds the moment he'd turned in the driveway. Once the motion sensors and alarms were deactivated, he reached into the car and collected the pizza, along with the plastic bag containing two six-packs of soda, one regular, one diet. "Come on in."

He headed for the side entrance, aware that Sydney hung back to give the place a once-over. He tried not to care that she'd see a house not unlike her own, with a bit of age on it, and a series of careful restorations designed to preserve the charm and character.

That's it, he thought with a slice of self-directed mockery, *charm and humor.* He didn't have much in the way of either, so he left that stuff up to his farmhouse.

He used his key to let them both through the side door, and quickly tapped his code into the security pad beside the door, telling the second level of protection to stand down.

When he turned, he found Sydney standing very near him in the small entryway, eyes shadowed with speculation. "Let me guess—this place has more surveillance gadgets than the average safe house."

He raised an eyebrow. "Are you implying that I'm paranoid?"

"No." She shook her head. "Guarded, maybe, but not paranoid. Besides," she quipped, "you know what they say about paranoids having enemies." Then her voice and expression turned serious, and she reached out to touch his arm, very fleetingly, through the material of his suit jacket and shirt. "What exactly is going on here?"

But he saw the heat in her eyes, and the acquiescence, and knew she felt the chemistry between them, too. "Don't ask the question if you already know the answer."

He very carefully, very deliberately, closed the distance between them and undid the straps of the Kevlar vest. After he'd stripped it away, he leaned in to kiss her.

She met him halfway.

Chapter Seven

It might've been the fear she'd lived with for so long that heated Sydney's blood and had her diving into Sharpe's kiss even though she knew it wasn't smart. It might've been loneliness that had her pressing up against him so they touched everywhere. It might've been too long spent without a man's touch, too long spent having to be in control, having to be on guard, that had her going pliant when he spun them and pressed her against the wall just inside the door.

Whatever the reasons, it was a hell of a kiss. And then some.

He filled her senses. Color and light burst behind her closed eyelids as she feasted on him, on the taste and smell of him, and the feel of his muscles beneath her fingertips. He was utterly, completely male, and as she felt him teeter on the razor-edge divide between control and wildness, she gloried in the knowledge that he felt the same way she did, needed the same thing she did.

The thought of Sharpe wanting her so badly he'd pull her out of the safe house just to have her to himself was as erotic as the kiss itself.

Blood thundered through her, knotting her muscles to needy fists as he pressed into her, grinding against her, all hard edges and raw male strength. She fought her way through the kiss, taking as much as giving, clutching his suit coat until the material crumpled beneath her grip, then letting go so she could run her hands beneath the jacket, along the crisp cotton of his shirt, and feel the man beneath.

When that wasn't enough, she gave in to the slide of his hand down her thigh and lifted both of her legs, wrapping them around his waist and hanging on for the ride.

He said something, the words coming out harsh and low, their meaning lost in another endless, soul-searching kiss. She pressed herself against him, glorying in the sensations: the rasp of late-day beard shadow along his jaw and the crisp material of his clothes and the hot, hard flesh beneath. Even the catch of her fingertips on his shoulder holster, and the hardness of the weapon itself were a turn-on. Who knew she was a sucker for a guy with a gun?

But she wasn't attracted to just any guy with a gun, Sydney knew deep inside. She was hooked on this one.

Sharpe had rescued her from Tiberius and his men. He'd sent people to help Celeste right away rather than using her sister as leverage. He was quick on his feet and even quicker with his mind; he not only kept up with her thought processes, half the time he was a step or two ahead of her. Even better, he was about a fifteen on a scale of one to hot, and he kissed like she'd fantasized he would, only better. What was not to like?

Warning bells sounded in the back of her brain, but they were quickly lost to a flare of heat as he banded a strong arm across her waist and spun away from the wall. He took two long strides—

And froze in place.

They drew apart and stared into each other's eyes, both breathing hard. Sydney's mind spun, and she imagined his was doing pretty much the same thing.

"Wow," she said after a long, still moment. "Wow. That was…"

"Not very smart." He relaxed his grip, letting her slide down his body as he fixed his attention on the wide-open door and the security panel, which he'd never reset. "I know. You're right."

"I was thinking unexpected, actually." It wasn't really; attraction had flared between them from the first. But she needed to say something other than *Let's lock the door and head upstairs,* because he was right. What they'd just done—and what undoubtedly would have followed if they hadn't pulled back—wasn't very smart at all.

"Unexpected works, too." But his attention wasn't on her as he crossed the room, shut the door and keyed in the security code. He was staring at the night outside, scanning the scene for signs of company.

"Nothing bad happened," she said, but knew that wasn't the point. While they'd been indulging in a little one-on-one, the door had been wide open, the security field down. It was only thanks to luck and circumstance that none of Tiberius's people had been outside to take advantage of the lapse.

His look said he knew she knew better, but true to form, instead of saying something redundant or unnecessary, he stayed silent.

He moved across the living room and looked down at the pizza. He picked up a soda, then set it down again. Without looking at her, he said, "I'm sorry. I'm not normally so impulsive. This attraction…" He waved a hand between the two of them. "Chemistry. Whatever it is, it's got me off stride. I'm all jumbled up, and I'm afraid I'm going to make a mistake because of it. I thought if we spent some time together, I could…I don't know, work it out in my head or something."

Suddenly, he wasn't the aloof, polished agent who spoke in clipped, precise sentences. In his place was someone who looked as frustrated as she felt, as his body told him one thing, his head another. The realization kindled a dangerous warmth in the vicinity of her heart.

"I know what you mean. Not exactly ideal circumstances for starting a—" she broke off and, correcting herself, said, "For getting involved."

"Go ahead and say it. Starting a relationship. That's where this seems to be headed, doesn't it?" He looked at her, and she got the feeling that he was baffled, and way outside his comfort zone.

"I don't know." She took one of the sodas, not to drink but so she'd have something in her hands, something to fiddle with. "The circumstances aren't exactly normal. Once you've got Tiberius in custody and have control of the viral sequence, and Celeste and I are cleared to start rebuilding our lives—and just stay with me on the optimism here, okay?—what's to say we'll still be interested in each other? This attraction might just be a situation-and-proximity thing."

"Do you think that's what it is?" His direct gaze caught her, forcing the truth.

"No," she said softly, nearly whispering. "I don't." Hadn't she been wishing all along that they'd met under different circumstances? Hadn't she thought they would've clicked if they'd met at a bar, or a bus stop or someplace equally mundane?

"Me neither."

They stared at each other for a long moment while the heat built and the urges deepened. Sydney's heart beat the tempo of *do it, do it, do it,* but she'd been incautious before and it'd cost her job, and put her in the position to make the wrong choice by going to work for Tiberius. She was determined not to make the wrong choice again. Not with something that felt like it could be important, if she let it be.

"We should wait," she said softly. "It's all too complicated right now."

"Yeah." He exhaled. "You're right. I know you're right."

"But…?" she asked, hearing it in his voice.

His grin went crooked. "I don't particularly want to wait."

"Me neither," she said, echoing his earlier words. But the tension lightened and the air between them thinned, and a bubble of nervous excitement expanded in her chest, because in agreeing that they were going to wait, they'd also agreed that there was something to wait for.

She didn't know what shape it would take, or how long it would last when it did happen, but it was something to look forward to. Something that went beyond Tiberius, who had been the focus of her life for far too long.

"So what now?" She glanced at the pizza, which he'd set on the low coffee table, and the alluring length of a long leather sofa on the other side. "Should we eat? Head back to the safe house?" *Go upstairs?* she was tempted to add, but didn't because she had a feeling he'd agree if she pushed, despite both of their better intentions.

Sharpe sighed. "It's just been a long bunch of days and I don't feel like getting right back on the road. I can hack the temptation if you can."

He sat on the sofa, flipped open one of the boxes and worked a piece of pizza onto a paper plate. He set the plate on the coffee table for her, shoved a soda beside it and put together a similar setup for himself. When he was done, he stripped off his suit jacket and slung it over the arm of a nearby chair, then tossed his holstered weapon atop it.

Then, balancing his pizza on his lap, he kicked off his shoes, put his feet up and leaned back on the sofa. Letting out a long sigh, he closed his eyes.

He was inviting her to relax with him, to be with him. To get to know him in a way she had a feeling few people did.

The sight of him stripped of some of the professional hard-ass veneer fascinated her, even as the sad lines beside his eyes and mouth, which didn't smooth out even in repose, tugged at her.

Telling herself that she could handle this—that she was an adult, they were both adults—she grabbed the plate and sat down beside him.

The couch gave under her weight, sliding her even closer to his warm bulk. She struggled for all of thirty seconds before she gave in, leaned against him and let her head fall naturally against the arm he'd thrown across the back of the couch.

After a brief pause, he sighed deeply and curled his arm around her.

They ate in silence as the old house settled in for the night around them. Unwilling to talk about what was happening between them, about Tiberius, or about how he planned to use the intel she'd given his teammates, Sydney finally said, "I like your house."

"Thanks." His smile held pure pleasure, along with acknowledgment of the neutral topic. "The previous owners 'modernized' and 'improved' the heck out of it," he said, sketching the words with one-handed finger quotes. "I bought it four years ago and have been picking away at it ever since. I'm not going all the way back to original, by any means. Outhouses are so 1800s, you know. But I'm going for the period feel."

"You're nailing it." She looked around, admiring the honey-toned wainscoting and wide-pine floors. They were king's boards, she knew, so-named because they were over twelve inches wide, and thus should've been saved for export to England prior to the Revolution. The staining around the sunken nailheads indicated that the boards were original, but their unnatural smoothness and high-gloss varnish were familiar signs from her own house, as were the faint encrustations of paint at the carved edges of the wainscoting. "Let me guess, they put down wall-to-wall, added another layer of paint to the eight already on the trim and pulled down the horse-hair plaster in favor of drywall."

His chuckle transmitted to her from the places where they pressed together, with her cheek on his shoulder and their torsos aligned. "There had to be a dozen layers of paint. One of them, I swear it was creosote or something. It was this nasty black color, and it took a good four rounds of paint stripper—and a couple of layers of skin—to get it off." He shuddered. "You can't imagine."

"Trust me, I can." She grinned. "Our dining room had a quarter-inch-thick layer of this awful middle-green color, like baby vomit or something."

Deep down inside she knew she shouldn't let herself lean. But he was so warm and solid against her, the weight of his arm such a comforting drape, that she found herself weakening and settling in, letting his warmth transmit to her and ease the places that had been so cold for so long.

While she was busy convincing herself that she could handle the attraction, that she could handle *him,* she fell asleep with her head tucked into the crook of his arm and her body nestled against his.

JOHN WAS IN SERIOUS trouble.

He held her close, watched her sleep and told himself he'd dodged a bullet when they'd agreed to wait, because he'd veered way out of his comfort zone and was speeding up, heading in the wrong direction.

Despite having brought her home on a whim, a compulsion, he didn't do flings, didn't do attractions that clicked too hard and hot, relationships that made no sense when he looked at them rationally. Worse, he wasn't doing much of anything rationally at the moment. If he was, he would've left her in the safe house. He would've stayed the hell away from her until it was absolutely, positively imperative that they share space, and then he would've kept his distance, interacting with her on a purely professional level.

Instead, he was in his own damn living room, cuddled up with her like this had been a date. And not even a first date, either. Their kiss might've had the passion of a new discovery, but their inconsequential small talk had been...

Hell, he didn't know what it'd been, other than so natural he'd fallen into it before he'd had time to think it through, and then once he had, once he realized he was teetering on the brink of another decision that'd fall squarely into the 'really stupid' category, he'd been too comfortable to move. He'd wound up watching her sleep.

And in doing so, he feared he'd already come too close to falling for her.

He knew the warning signs. Hell, he'd been in that place once before, with a woman who was at once completely unlike Sydney and very like her, and in a very similar situation—one that should've taught him not to go there ever again.

So why had he?

Maybe he had a white knight complex. Yeah, he thought, that was it. The others might think him too cold and unemotional, but somewhere deep inside he had a big old rescue fantasy that played out in his choice of women. Of course, being who he was, he couldn't have a typical white knight complex, one where he fell for damsels in distress who needed a big, strong man to fix their problems. No, that would've been too easy. He had to be attracted to the ones who didn't want to be rescued. Yep, that played. He was—and had always been—all about making his own life as difficult as possible.

Which didn't do a thing to cool his ardor when Sydney made a small noise and cuddled closer.

His flesh tightened and his blood buzzed in his veins, and for a moment he imagined himself waking her up with a kiss, pulling her against him, rolling her beneath him, pressing them both into the soft, yielding sofa cushions. Worse, he could see himself with her a week from now, a month from now. He wanted to argue with her, trade barbs with her, sink himself into her and let the world go hang itself.

And none of those feelings were real, he knew. They were illusions, his own internal construct of what affection was supposed to feel like.

He'd thought he was in love once before, and had later learned it was all a lie.

"I can't do this," he whispered against her temple, his breath stirring the fine hairs that had fallen across her lovely face.

"Mmm?" She stirred against him, frowning as though fighting consciousness when fantasies were so much better.

He didn't repeat himself.

"I said it's time to get going." He nudged her awake. "If we're gone much longer, Grace is going to send SWAT out after us." That was an overstatement—he'd checked in with the computer specialist an hour ago—but they couldn't stay where they were.

His place might be safe from Tiberius, but he was quickly learning that spending time alone with Sydney carried other, equally dangerous risks.

"Come on. Rise and shine." He got her up and moving despite her sleepy protests, and loaded her in his car. She slept most of the way back to the safe house, which was a relief, but she'd begun to wake up on her own by the time they were a few miles out.

She yawned and stretched, the motion pulling her cheeky red sweater tight across her breasts in a way he couldn't force himself to ignore—especially not after having experienced her body firsthand.

Their kiss was something he feared his brain would keep on instant recall for far too long.

Jaw set, John forced himself to face front and keep driving. "You should put the Kevlar back on."

He hadn't seen any signs of pursuit, but he also wasn't taking any chances. This was Tiberius they were talking about, and the criminal businessman didn't believe in losing. He also didn't believe in loose ends.

He would come after Sydney—it was inevitable. That left it up to John and his team to try to control the when and where, and hope to hell they got it right.

He hadn't used her as bait tonight, but that didn't mean he might not be forced to do just that in the near future. The very thought of it chilled him, made him want to pull her close and promise her impossible things.

Instead, he waved to the surveillance team sitting in a darkened car on the street outside the safe house as he drove past, and hit the button to open the door of the safe house's attached garage.

He'd phoned Grace from the road to check that everything was status quo, and had gotten the all-clear. He called through again once they were in the garage, using the pre-arranged signal, and got the proper counterpassword in return, indicating that it was safe to bring Sydney inside.

"Come on." He didn't draw his weapon, but stayed close to her on the way into the house, just in case. Once they were inside he took the lead, heading for the kitchen. "Grace hinted earlier that she was closing in on something. Maybe she's got something that'll—"

He broke off at the sight that confronted him.

Impressions came to him in strobe-quick flashes: Grace bound to a kitchen chair, head lolling in a drug-induced stupor, her computer trashed and two thugs standing behind her, weapons at the ready.

Before John could react, one of them shot Grace in the temple, execution style.

Grace! John had his gun in his hand seconds later and opened fire, his brain short-circuiting on rage and sick horror as his teammate collapsed sideways, her mouth askew, her eyes glazing in death.

His first bullet caught Gracie's murderer in the upper chest, spinning the gunman away from her and sending him to his knees in a spray of blood. The second guy ducked and bolted out of the kitchen and through the back door.

For a second John was torn between his imperative to guard his protectee, and the all-consuming need to gun down the bastard who'd just killed his teammate.

Then he heard something that made the decision for him: the crash of breaking glass sounded in the front room, followed by a thump and the sound of a metal object rolling across the hardwood floor.

Grenade, his brain supplied. He didn't know if it was a flash-bang or gas, but he wasn't sticking around to find out.

Walling the grief and shock off in a small corner of his consciousness, he snapped to agent mode, processing and rejecting his available choices. He didn't dare go out the kitchen door; it was a sure bet the second gunman would be waiting, his need to finish the job no doubt fueled by the knowledge of what had happened to the last pair of killers to fail Tiberius.

That really left only one option: they had to go down.

In a reflex arc that didn't even make it to his brain before he was on the move, John grabbed Sydney and dragged her across the kitchen, past Grace and the small blood pool gathering beneath her chair. He yanked open the door that led to the basement. "Come on!"

The lights flickered on the moment the door opened, showing a set of plain wooden stairs. He charged down them, hauling Sydney along as the seconds ticked down in his head.

Behind and above him, there were more thump-roll sounds, followed by the boom of a flash-bang stun grenade, the powerful noise muted by walls and distance.

It wasn't the flash-bangs that had him moving fast, though. He had to assume the additional sounds were gas canisters. It only made sense, because Tiberius didn't want to blow Sydney up; he wanted her alive, and in his power.

And that so wasn't going to happen if John had anything to say about it. Heart hammering in his ears, jaw
set in determination, he had only one goal right now: to
get Sydney out alive.

After that, it was war.

The basement was a cement cube containing a furnace and water heater but none of the usual basement
clutter, because nobody actually lived in the safe house
year-round. In addition to the electrical panel and other
basement stuff, there was a door set in the wall opposite
the furnace. John yanked it open, revealing a low,
cement-lined tunnel.

The air in the basement had already started to turn
with the first whiff of the gas, suggesting that Tiberius's
men were using one of the newer cocktails, which
readily diffused down, as well as up. Worse, footsteps
sounded from above, indicating that the men had
donned masks rather than waiting for the air to clear.
Any moment now, they'd figure out that their quarry had
gone to ground.

Muffled shouts and the quickening tramp overhead
signaled they already had.

"Go!" John pushed Sydney ahead of him. Once they
were both inside the tunnel, he yanked the heavy door
shut and spun the lock, then urged her along the tunnel
ahead of him. "Hurry!"

He was less worried about the men following through
the tunnel, and more worried that they'd quickly figure
out where it led.

The lights had come up when he'd opened the door.
The thin fluorescent strips, which were hung on either

side of the low cement tunnel, lit the way as they scrambled along. They had to crouch down, bent nearly double as they moved as fast as they could on their feet, hands, knees, whatever part of them could keep the forward momentum going.

Sydney didn't say a word, just kept going as the walls closed in on them and the air started to carry a whiff of gas that had John's head spinning. Her jaw was set, her skin very pale and he had a feeling her brain was jammed—as was his—on the sight of Grace tied to a kitchen chair, shot dead with a bullet in her brain.

How in the hell had that happened?

He'd checked in regularly. Hell, he'd even checked in from the garage. What had gone wrong? How had Tiberius found the safe house? How had his men gotten past the security system, and the surveillance teams who were supposed to be keeping watch from the outside?

Knowing that the others teams might also be dead, John felt his heart chill in his chest, felt something wither up and die within him. He stumbled and went down, the gas-tainted fumes sapping his strength, but he forced himself to struggle up and keep going, shoving Sydney ahead of him.

"There should be a door," he said, hearing his breath rattle in his lungs.

"I don't—" she said weakly, then gave a low cry. "There's a turn up ahead. Maybe that's it."

It wasn't, but once they made the turn they could see the door at the end of the tunnel, which sloped slightly upward until it ended in a metal slab that was twin to the one they'd entered through. Shuffling in their awkward crouches, laboring to suck tainted air into their cramped lungs, they hurried to the door. Sydney fumbled to unlock it, and for a frozen second John feared it was jammed on the other side, that Tiberius's men had already beaten them to the neighboring house, which was also owned by the government for use as a safe house and as an escape route.

"Got it!" She finally got the lock open, twisted the handle and moved to shove open the door.

"Wait." John grabbed her. "Me first." He couldn't let them make a foolish mistake in the mad rush to escape the bad air. Crowding past her so he led the way, weapon at the ready, he tried to gather his scrambled brain cells and cracked open the door.

For a second there was nothing but blackness. Then the swing of the door triggered the basement lights and they clicked on to reveal…nothing.

The basement was as empty as the one they'd just left. Even better, he didn't detect movement on the floor above, and the air was clean, though faintly humid with typical cellar dampness.

"Come on." Moving fast, he got her out of the tunnel and shut the door, then crossed to the stairs. He put a finger to his lips to caution silence, and they crept up the stairs with him in the lead and her breathing down the back of his neck, both of them trying not to make a sound.

Tension hummed through him. Fear, not that he'd be hurt—that was part of the job description—but that he might not be quick enough or good enough to keep the woman behind him safe.

He'd failed Grace. He didn't want to fail Sydney.

Tightening his grip on his weapon, he paused at the top of the stairs and flicked off the lights.

Sydney stiffened behind him. For a second he thought it was because of the darkness, or the shock settling in to her system. Then he heard it, too.

Footsteps.

He had a split second to consider his options, which were seriously slim. They couldn't go back into the tunnel because of the foul air, and because Tiberius's men could block them in from either end. There was another way out of the basement—a set of stairs leading to a traditional bulkhead—but odds were good that if Tiberius's people had discovered the second empty house, they had the grounds covered, too. That left him with going through the house itself.

The layout was identical to that of the house Sydney had been staying in, the furniture and placement nearly identical, as well. The footsteps were coming from the left of their current position. To the right, there should be a short hallway that dead-ended in a bathroom, with a spare room to the right. To the left of the basement door, there was another entryway leading to the kitchen, which ran the length of the back of the house.

The only thing that was different about the two houses was the garage placement. The first house had an attached garage on the left from the street-level perspective. The second had an almost identical garage, but on the right.

It was, perhaps, their one advantage.

Thinking fast, John put his lips very near Sydney's ear, and breathed, "When I open the door I want you to turn right and head through the kitchen. There's a door next to the refrigerator—go through it, and close and lock it behind you. You'll be in the garage. There should be a car in there. The keys are under the visor, along with the door remote. Get out of here." He palmed his cell phone and handed it to her. "I'll call you when it's over."

"But—"

"Don't," he interrupted. "Don't try to be a hero or back me up or anything. You'll just be in the way."

He could see the arguments in her eyes, could see the indecision, the desire to be brave warring with basic self-preservation. "Okay," she said finally. Then she turned her face so her lips touched his. "Please be careful."

The brief kiss shouldn't have warmed him, shouldn't have soothed him, shouldn't have mattered to him. But because it did warm and soothe and matter, he drew back, going for cool and in control when his heart was hammering in his chest.

"Take care of yourself," he said urgently. "Keep driving until I call—stay on busy roads where people can see you. If the men see you and follow you out, they'll be more likely to hang back if there are witnesses." He hoped. Right then, it was the best he could do.

She nodded, then stiffened.

Beyond the door, the footsteps drew closer and then hesitated, as though their owner had seen the light beneath the basement door.

John took three quick breaths, steadied himself to kill and opened the door.

He swung out and to the left, weapon at the ready, while Sydney broke right and ran for her life.

Chapter Eight

Sydney lunged down to the hallway and through the kitchen, heart hammering in her ears and breath whistling in her lungs. Her legs shook with fear and adrenaline, but she forced them to carry her. Nearly sobbing with fear, she yanked open the door to the garage and plunged through.

She skidded to a halt.

The garage door was open. A man stood silhouetted in the opening, waiting for her.

A scream locked her throat, driving the breath from her body, and all she could think was that Tiberius had found her. He'd take her somewhere, torture her and then kill her once she gave up the password. It was over. Her mistakes had come home to damn her.

"No!" she screamed, refusing to believe, refusing to give in. She scrambled back through the kitchen door and into the house, bolting toward Sharpe as if he could help her, as if he could—

"Sydney!" a voice called from behind her. "Wait up! It's okay!"

She'd barely processed the words when she slammed into Sharpe coming the other way.

He let out an *oof* of surprise but weathered the impact, and his arms came up to hold her tight, to keep her from running. "It's okay," he said, echoing the other man's reassurance. "They're the good guys."

He had to repeat the words several times before they penetrated her overwrought brain. When they did, when she actually looked around herself and saw SWAT garb and badges, the fight went out of her like someone had yanked her plug, cutting off her power.

She sagged against Sharpe and burst into tears.

He caught her automatically, but there was little warmth in the embrace, as though he didn't want the others to see, didn't want them to guess at the relationship that might—or might not—be developing between them.

"Sorry." She drew away, sniffing mightily and swiping at her eyes.

"You're entitled." But his voice and expression were cool, making him look like an entirely different person than the one she'd been with the night before. This was Special Agent Sharpe, not the man she'd cuddled with on his couch.

"Sorry," she said again, backing off, then again, inanely, "I'm sorry."

She didn't even know precisely what she was apologizing for, except that all of this was her fault. Tiberius's men had come because of her. Grace had—

"Oh, God." Her eyes widened and she lifted her hands to her mouth to hold in the surge of emotion and bile that slapped at her the moment she thought of what had happened in the other house, all because of her. *"Grace!"*

"Yeah, I know." A flare of emotion crossed Sharpe's face, regret and pain and anger, but instead of moving toward Sydney in comfort, he took a step away. He gestured to two of the SWAT members. "Escort her to your van, please, and keep her there until I come for her."

"Yes, sir." They didn't salute, but they might as well have, because they snapped into action and hustled her down the hallway to the side door, and from there to the street, forcing her to keep her head down and move fast as they surrounded her with their bodies.

Sydney caught a glimpse of curious onlookers gathering in a range of nightwear and at-home casual clothes. Both of the safe houses were ablaze with light, and the first house bristled with the mechanics of murder—officers and evidence techs, and the other members of Sharpe's team, their faces etched with shock and grief, horror and rage.

I did this, Sydney thought, going numb to her soul. She hadn't wielded the hammer that'd broken Jenny Marie's fingers and she hadn't shoved the young woman off an island cliff. She hadn't pulled the trigger of the weapon that had killed Danielle and Jay. She hadn't pumped Grace full of whatever drug had loosened her enough to provide Sharpe with the "all clear" password when the situation had been far from all clear, and she hadn't shot Grace in the temple.

But ultimately she was responsible for all those things. Tiberius was sending her the same message he'd sent her once before: *don't mess with me or I'll destroy the things you care about.*

She'd gotten Celeste out of his reach—God willing—but that hadn't stopped him from killing Grace, the only woman Sydney had been friendly with since Jenny Marie's death. Which meant anyone else she was even the slightest bit close to was in terrible danger.

"Step up," said one of the SWAT team members, a fortysomething guy with salt-shot dark hair and kind-seeming gray eyes.

Sydney blanked. "What?"

He indicated the SWAT van. "Climb in. You'll be safe in here while we get the scene secure."

"Oh. Right." She climbed aboard and found herself in a utilitarian rear compartment with sideways-facing bench seats and racks and lockers holding a variety of equipment. But as she sat on the long, uncomfortable metal bench, she realized he'd been right, whether he'd meant it that way or not. She needed to step up and start taking responsibility for her actions.

Jenny Marie had died because Sydney had used her to get information to Celeste. Danielle and Jay had died because she hadn't been smart enough when she escaped, hadn't been quick enough at getting them help. Grace had died because she hadn't given the team enough to go on, enough to justify a raid and an arrest. Four people were dead, indirectly because of her.

Sydney dropped her face into her hands. It was too much to bear.

"Hey."

Recognizing Sharpe's voice, she looked up quickly. Despite everything else, despite the situation and the danger, and the horror she'd just endured, a little jolt of electricity sped her heartbeat at the sight of him standing in the open van doors, staring at her.

His dark hair was mussed, his jaw heavily shadowed with stubble, and he still had his discarded tie wadded up in the pocket of his tired-looking button-down shirt. Beneath the gray suit jacket she could see the straps of his shoulder holster, which he'd put back on before they left his house.

He looked sexy as hell, and lethally cold. She'd never realized before how much of a turn-on the combination could be until she'd met him. Until she'd kissed him and realized that the agent's cool exterior camouflaged a warm, caring man. One she liked and trusted.

One she wanted. And that was a big problem, because if Tiberius had known about the safe house, and about Grace, then he knew about Sharpe, as well.

Which meant the agent was as much—if not more—of a target than she was.

I'll kill them, Tiberius was saying. *I'll kill the people around you, and I'll keep killing them until you give me the password.*

"Hey," she said, smiling faintly. "I'm glad you—"

"I just wanted to get my phone," he cut in. "Then I've got to get back to work."

I wasn't going to get mushy, she wanted to say, but there were other people around, so she didn't. Instead, picking her words carefully, she said, "Did something else happen I should know about?"

She didn't think his banked anger was all about Grace and the attack on the safe house. Not that he didn't have a right to be angry about those things, but this anger seemed more specific. More directed at her, like she'd done something truly terrible.

He looked at her and she nearly shivered at the contempt in his expression. "Don't bother. The game's up."

Her blood chilled in her veins. "What game? What's going on?" She reached out to touch him but he moved away. "What are you talking about?"

He looked at her long and hard, and she couldn't read a thing from his expression. Finally, he said, "Grace managed to get a message off to Jimmy before they grabbed her. It turns out I was right. There was someone on the inside working for Tiberius. It just wasn't who I suspected it would be."

He pulled a folded sheet of paper from the inner pocket of his suit coat and passed it to her.

Heart thundering in her ears, Sydney unfolded the page and scanned the contents. It was an e-mail message, sent from a Hotmail account she didn't recognize. She recognized the destination, though. It was one of the accounts held by Tiberius Corp. One of the ones she'd used during their early negotiations about her coming to work on the island.

The message was simple and damning. It gave the location of the safe house and the positions of the surveillance teams, ending with *I trust you'll live up to your end of the bargain.* It was signed with the same initials that were in the hotmail address: SEW.

Sydney Ellen Westlake.

Her fingers went numb and the paper fluttered to the floor of the SWAT van. "I didn't send that message. That isn't my e-mail account."

"What was the deal?" he said, as though he hadn't heard her. Or maybe he'd heard her and had already judged her and found her guilty. The utter disgust in his expression certainly suggested as much.

His mistrust cut Sydney straight to the quick. So much for them being on the same page regarding the attraction between them. If he was this ready to believe the worst of her, then he wasn't the man she'd thought he was.

Anger flared. Hurt. Confusion. "Where is this coming from?" she said softly. "Why won't you listen? I've done everything you've asked. I'm cooperating."

"Yes, but with whom?" He retrieved the paper, reread the contents. His voice was coldly conversational when he said, "What did he promise you, freedom? Safety? Access to your records so you could complete the cure for your sister? More money than you could spend in this lifetime?"

"He already promised me all that," Sydney snapped, anger coming to the forefront. "And I still took my life into my own hands and escaped from the island because I refused to be involved in building a bioweapon."

"All evidence to the contrary." He folded the paper and returned it to his pocket.

"It's a fake." Her volume increased, earning curious looks from outside the van. "I'm telling you, I didn't write the e-mail. It's not my account!"

"Grace checked that. The message traced back to the IP address on her laptop at the safe house." He paused. "What did you do, wait until she was asleep and sneak access? How'd you get around the firewalls? Something your sister taught you?"

"I didn't," she said miserably, anger losing steam as

the heartache built. "I didn't sneak Grace's computer to e-mail Tiberius and I sure as hell didn't tell him where the safe house was located. I didn't." Her shoulders sagged. "I swear. You have to believe me."

But there was no belief in his cold blue eyes, no compassion. And there was no hesitation when he turned and walked away.

JOHN STOOD on the sidelines while the evidence techs did their thing in the kitchen where Grace had died. He knew his strengths, and crime scene reconstruction wasn't one of them. Besides, he didn't need to reconstruct a damn thing. He'd been there. He'd witnessed it.

He couldn't get the sight of Grace's face out of his head, even after the techs had bagged and tagged the body and transported it away from the scene. John had lost team members before—life-threatening danger was, unfortunately, part of the job description in the major crimes unit—but he'd never before been up close and personal with premeditated murder during the actual act.

She'd been executed not ten feet away from him, which made it impossible for him not to think about what he should've done differently, and there, the answer was simple.

He should never have left the scene with Sydney. He shouldn't have taken her home, shouldn't have spent time with her alone when he could've been working instead.

While he and Sydney had been cuddling on the couch, Tiberius's hired guns had been taking out the surveillance teams—drugging them rather than killing them, thankfully—and subduing Grace. While he and Sydney had been driving back to the safe house, Tiberius's men had bound Grace and pumped her full of God only knew what for questioning.

She would've held out as long as she could, and when she broke under the combination of chemicals and interrogation—maybe worse, he didn't know yet—she would've given them as little as possible.

He hoped like hell she'd been too far gone to realize she'd given the countersigns that would lead him into the trap. He hated thinking that she'd died knowing she'd failed her team leader.

It's okay, Grace, he said inside his own skull, in case her spirit lingered nearby, or maybe because he needed to say it for himself.

Only it wasn't okay. It was far from okay.

How had he not known Sydney was still in contact with Tiberius? He should've sensed that was where her head was at, should've known she'd try something like this.

History repeated. Back at the university where she'd worked before, she'd tried to pressure the administration to reinstate her funding by accusing her ex-lover of stealing some of her work. Combine that with her decision to work with Tiberius despite knowing at least something of what he was, and there was a pattern of unaccountability. Why had he thought she'd changed?

Because you wanted her, his baser self said. And damn it, that part of him was right. He'd overlooked the history because after watching her with her sister, he'd convinced himself she'd done what she'd done out of love, and because she'd felt like she was out of other options. That didn't make it right, but it was understandable to a point.

But this…this was inexcusable. Unforgivable.

"Hey." Jimmy Oliverra came up beside John, gave him a nod and took position beside him, leaning back against the wall in a section of kitchen that'd already been processed for evidence. "They saying anything yet?"

Jimmy was the major crime unit's secondary—and now, John supposed, their primary—computer whiz. He'd spent the most time of any of them working shoulder-to-shoulder with Grace, and the grief showed in his eyes and the deep lines beside his mouth. He was a professional, though. He'd soldier on despite—or perhaps because of—the emotions.

John knew he needed to do the same, and it rattled him to know he needed the reminder.

You're the Iceman, he told himself. *Pull it together.*

"They haven't found anything we didn't already know or guess," he said, answering Jimmy's question about the evidence techs. "And we're not going to change that by sitting here and staring at them." He turned for the door. "Let's go."

Jimmy hesitated. "Can I have a minute? I'd like to…you know, say goodbye."

John didn't bother pointing out that they'd already transported the body. He nodded. "Make it quick."

AN HOUR LATER, the major crimes unit was assembled in a conference room deep within Quantico. Sydney was in a "guest" room down the hall, with a locked door that assured she was going nowhere until John was good and ready for her to leave.

He'd had it with working around her. This time, she was going to give them everything, or he'd nail her with obstruction, conspiracy and whatever else he could think of.

"She's got immunity," Jimmy reminded him when he muttered something to that effect.

John glared. "Not anymore she doesn't. That e-mail voids the immunity agreement. Period."

There was silence from the four teammates assembled around the table. Jimmy sat next to John. On the other side sat sharpshooter Michael Pelotti and Drew Dietz, their evidence specialist. There was an empty chair between Drew and Michael, where Grace would've sat.

John felt her loss keenly. She'd been the one to sometimes soften his rough edges, the one who'd challenged him to tread the middle ground.

Then again, the middle ground had gotten them where they were now. Maybe it was time for a take-no-prisoners type of approach.

"She might be telling the truth," Michael said, his tone thoughtful, like the man himself. Dark and lean, the sharpshooter spoke the way he fired—smoothly and deliberately. "Tiberius is clever. If he figured out he could use Sydney to put you off your game, he'd do it in a heartbeat."

"I'm not off my game," John growled. "I'm fine."

But Michael had known him a long time, longer than the others. "I don't think she's working for him, to be honest. I just don't see it. Think about it for a second—

Tiberius could have looked into your background, found out about the other incident and figured a fake e-mail implicating Sydney would be a good way to push your buttons. Even if it didn't, he could be assured you'd throw out her intel the moment you suspected she was still working for him. That'd push back any plan for raiding the island. Maybe that was his goal."

"You're giving him too much credit," John said. But he couldn't totally dismiss the possibility. First, because he trusted Michael as much as he trusted anyone, and the sharpshooter was leaning toward Sydney's side, and second because, damn it, despite his knee-jerk fury when he'd first seen the e-mail, the more time passed the less likely he found the whole scenario.

Sydney had said it herself. She'd risked her life to lock down her work and escape from Rocky Cliff Island. With her sister safe and an immunity deal in place, what leverage could possibly compel her to accept another offer from Tiberius? She knew what happened to his loose ends. There was no way she would've believed he'd let her walk away once it was all over.

Which suggested she was innocent—of the e-mail, at least.

"So what's the plan?" Jimmy asked. There were deep shadows beneath the computer tech's eyes, and his shoulders sagged under the weight of his grief. The youngest and newest member of the group, he hadn't experienced the loss of a teammate before, and Grace's death had hit him hard.

"Whether or not the e-mail is a fake," John said, trying to reorient his brain and make a new set of decisions on the fly, "and I'm not willing to say one way or the other right now, it was good enough to fool Grace. It should be enough to get permission for a raid, especially coupled with the other intel we've managed to accumulate."

That got everyone's attention. Michael said carefully, "What other intel?" His real question was obvious: why didn't we know about it?

John spread his hands. "Sorry for the secrecy, but this was really need-to-know stuff from one of the other teams working Tiberius." And he wasn't the only one who suspected there was a leak, not in his team, but somewhere higher up the chain of command. The team leaders were keeping a very tight hold on their information as the case developed.

"And?" Jimmy prompted.

John said, "There's been some serious chatter between the island and reps of four other major players." He named three of the country's ranking mob bosses and a wealthy importer who specialized in drugs from south of the border. All four had recently been indicted and were awaiting trial, three for murder, one for rape.

All four of the cases hinged on DNA evidence.

Michael whistled. "He's lining up his buyers. Does that mean he's cracked the computers?"

"Unknown." John scrubbed his hands across his face and heard stubble rasp.

Exhaustion beat at him. He'd been up for... Hell, he'd lost track of how long it'd been since he last slept. He needed to rest; they all did. But there was no way he was letting Tiberius get away with what he appeared to be planning.

"I've looked at the programs," Jimmy said, making a visible effort to focus on the conversation. "They're good. Better than good, even. But they're not uncrackable."

"Could you break them?" Michael asked.

"Under a deadline? Fifty-fifty," Jimmy said. "But given enough time and firepower, yeah. I think I could."

"So if he's contacting buyers, odds are that he thinks his people are close to breaking the code," John said.

"Or he was counting on getting his hands on Sydney during tonight's attack," Michael countered.

In the ensuing pause, Drew spoke up. "Not to be a total buzz kill, but how do you know he doesn't already have Sydney's viral vector? What if he was contacting the buyers to set up payment and drop points?"

John shook his head automatically. "He doesn't have the bug yet. If he did, he would've left Rocky Cliff. There's no way he's staying there long-term. He's too vulnerable there. We know too much about the defenses, and he knows we…" He trailed off, realizing what he'd just said. "Oh, hell."

The logic played, which meant Tiberius didn't have the bug…and Sydney hadn't sent the e-mail.

If she were working with Tiberius again, and had asked him to break her out of the safe house, then she would've already given him the password. He wouldn't have committed his forces without that assurance.

Ergo, Sydney hadn't sent the e-mail. Somebody else within the organization had done so.

And he'd refused to listen to her claims of innocence.

Like the cold SOB they called him, he'd automatically assumed the worst of her.

"Is it possible to send something from one computer and make it look like it came from another?" he asked Jimmy.

The tech didn't even hesitate, as though he'd been thinking along the same lines. "Yes, if you use one of those remote uplink programs, the ones that let you dial in to your home computer and use your own on-screen desktop and stuff from a remote location. It's conceivable that someone could hack in and send an e-mail that looked like it came from Grace's laptop, under a Hotmail account they'd set up using Sydney's initials, without ever touching the machine."

"Which could mean this doesn't involve anyone on the inside," Michael observed.

"Not necessarily." John tried to talk himself out of it, but couldn't see any other way. "There has to be someone working for Tiberius, not on the team or surveillance, necessarily, but somewhere in the network. There's no other way he could've known not only the address of the safe house, but also the surveillance posts. Also, they knew they needed to get a second counterpassword from Grace. There's no way they would've known that without a heads-up. I just can't see Grace volunteering the info, regardless of what hell they put her through. She was too good an agent for that."

There was a moment of uncomfortable silence before Drew said, "So what's the plan?"

"I can only see one choice," John said finally. "We

can't risk Tiberius getting the bug into circulation. We're going to have to raid the island."

"Think you can get it sanctioned?" Michael asked.

"More or less," John answered. "I'll call in a few favors, collect an insertion team I trust and get permission on the hush-hush. I can't help thinking if we do this all the way through official channels, Tiberius is going to be a step ahead of us the whole way through." He paused. "We might even think of filtering some misinformation through a few channels, and see what comes back. It'd give us an idea where the leak is coming from."

Jimmy nodded. "Drew and I will come up with some suggestions."

Michael, who was the muscle of the group, and the one with the most combat training, said, "Give me names and I'll get with the insertion team." He paused. "Are we using the intel from Sydney?"

John nodded. "Yeah. Use it. Get back to me with any questions." He paused. "Anything else?"

There were negative headshakes all around.

"Okay." John stood, body as tense as if he were going into battle. "I'll be back in a few minutes. I owe Sydney an apology."

AFTER AN HOUR or so sitting alone in the drab conference room, Sydney's tears had dried and she'd stripped out of the heavy, uncomfortable Kevlar vest. She folded it and used it as a pillow as she tried to nap while leaning on the conference table, but the bulletproof vest didn't rank very high in the comfort department and she couldn't calm her brain enough for sleep.

Every time she closed her eyes she saw Grace's face. And when she wasn't picturing the murder, she was imagining handcuffs and a jail cell, because there was no doubt in her mind that was where she was headed next. If Sharpe believed she'd sent that e-mail, he wouldn't hesitate to tear up the immunity agreement.

The more she thought about it, the more she was convinced that was what was going to happen next. So much so that when the door swung open, she shot to her feet, expecting cops with handcuffs and chains.

It wasn't the cops. It was Sharpe.

Her first thought was that he looked tired, her second that even tired, he looked incredible. And the latter made her angry, because how dare he look so good when she was miserable, and how dare her body still react to him when he'd just proved he'd always think the worst of her, despite her protests to the contrary.

She lifted her chin and glared at him. "I. Did. Not. Send. That. E-mail."

"I know," he said quietly. "I'm sorry I didn't listen to you before."

It took her a second to process the words, longer to comprehend their meaning. When she did, the images of handcuffs and chains vanished and she collapsed into her chair. "You know?" The question came out small and quivery, but on the heels of relief came a flare of anger. She regained her feet. "Well, good. And you *should* be sorry. You should've believed me. You can't say you're interested in me one minute, and then think the worst of me in the next. It's not fair."

She half expected him to tell her it was all off, that

he'd rethought the idea of them being together and decided it was a bad idea, that he didn't want her enough to deal with the complications. And in a way that might've been a relief, because it'd take the decision out of her hands and give her a reason to hate him instead of wishing for things that seemed impossible.

But instead of saying it was over before it'd even begun, he spun one of the chairs so it faced hers, and sat, gesturing for her to do the same.

When she was seated, he said, "You're absolutely right—I should have listened to you, and I shouldn't have jumped to conclusions."

She regarded him warily. "What changed your mind?"

"We—well, Jimmy and Michael, really—stepped back and looked at that e-mail, and finally figured out that the logic doesn't add up. Someone—most likely Tiberius or someone working for him—was trying to make you look guilty in order to complicate things at this end."

She wrinkled her nose. "Gee, you think?"

He exhaled. "I should probably explain what happened back there." He paused. "I was involved a few years ago…with someone who was part of a case."

That was so not what she'd been expecting, that it took her a moment to reorient. She also had to breathe past a hot knot of something that wasn't quite anger, wasn't quite jealousy. When she'd settled the uneasy churn in her gut, she said, "Grace mentioned that you'd been involved with a witness."

"A witness." He grimaced. "I guess that's an accurate term, albeit a kind one. Her name was Rose." He paused, and for a moment she didn't think he was going to keep going. Then, as though reaching a decision, he exhaled a long breath. "We'd been working as part of a multi-agency task force trying to bring down a major criminal working out of Boston. His name was Viggo Trehern, and he was seriously bad news. The task force had managed to get three people on the inside pretty early on—a woman who went under as Trehern's mistress, the doctor who handled his addiction to prescription meds and one of his enforcers. It wasn't my call, but none of them knew about the others, so when it went bad, it went bad fast. The woman died, the doctor's cover was broken and the enforcer dropped out of sight for a while. We needed another way in."

"Rose," Sydney said. It wasn't a question.

He nodded. "Rose. It was my job to find the weak link. I did my homework, and picked the most likely candidate for turning. She'd been Tiberius's lover, but was a good enough cook that when he got tired of her in his bed, he kept her in the kitchen. We watched her for a few weeks, got her patterns down, and I arranged to bump into her at a nightclub near the theater district."

"You seduced her to get her on your side?" Sydney said, suddenly not liking this story at all.

"No." He shook his head in an emphatic negative. "We were friends, nothing more. She was a good person stuck in a bad situation, and I gave her a way out. A deal. Immunity for information."

Sydney's stomach did a nasty little shimmy. "Suddenly this is sounding way too familiar."

"I know. I'm sorry." He paused. "Her tips were good,

and suddenly we were making more progress against Trehern than we'd ever managed before. After a few smaller takedowns, the task force leaders trusted her— I trusted her—and based on her information, we planned to close the net on Trehern for good. There was no way we were letting him wiggle out this time. We had everything sewn up tight. I thought—" He broke off and grimaced. "We had talked about after, about there maybe being a future for us."

The shimmy edged toward full-on nausea at the parallels. "Go on."

"It probably doesn't take a brilliant research scientist to guess she double-crossed me...us. She'd been working for Trehern all along, feeding us whatever tidbits of information he wanted us to have, leading us straight into a trap. If it weren't for the one remaining guy we had on the inside, the enforcer, William Caine, the whole thing would've gone to hell. As it was, I lost two good men and the total casualty count in the task force was in the dozens. We got Trehern, but the cost was high. Too high."

And he blamed himself for the deaths, Sydney realized. As far as he was concerned, those agents had died because he'd trusted the wrong woman.

The knowledge definitely helped explain his reaction to the phony e-mail. But just as definitely, it set off serious warning bells. "I've got to tell you, I'm a little freaked out by the similarities."

"Trust me, you're not the only one."

"Did you..." She paused, trying to figure out what she really wanted to know. "Did you feel the same way about her that you feel about me?"

He took her hands in his. "God help me, I don't know the answer to that."

It wasn't what she'd wanted to hear. But one thing she knew about him was that he'd never tell her what she wanted to hear, just for the sake of placating her.

At the moment, his honesty was cold comfort.

"I wasn't brought up with a whole lot of affection," he continued, "and this isn't exactly a job that encourages touchy-feeliness. Rose brought out something in me that I wasn't used to. Something I liked. And yes, you make me feel some of the same things, but it's different. *You're* different."

"Right. Because I'm not still working for Tiberius."

He squeezed her hands in his and moved closer still. "It's more than that. You're…more of a whole person than Rose was. You're out there, making things happen. Not always the right thing, granted, but you're trying to fix what you did wrong. I admire that, even if I don't always agree with your methods."

"Was there a compliment in there somewhere?" Sydney asked. "I couldn't tell." But she felt herself softening.

She told herself not to forgive him this easily, but she could already tell it was a losing battle. He believed her. Wasn't that enough?

"Yeah." His chuckle sounded tired. "I think so. There should've been, anyway." He crowded closer, still holding her hands. Their knees bumped together and his eyes were very close to hers, and if she'd wanted to—if she'd been ready to after what'd just happened between them—she could've leaned in and kissed him.

But she didn't. She couldn't. Not after what had just happened, what she'd just learned.

"Can I trust you not to knee-jerk believe the worst of me again?" she asked quietly. "I don't want to be involved in…whatever this is, if I'm going to be constantly on the defensive. Is it enough for me to tell you, here and now, that I'm on your side? That I won't do anything to compromise you or the team?"

"Even if it means destroying your work on the island?" he countered.

She closed her eyes on a flash of pain, but nodded. "Even if that's what it means." Opening her eyes, she stared into his, willing him to believe her. "Celeste did okay without me. Better than okay, really. If she has to wait another year or two for me to scrape up the funding and replicate the work, I think she can manage it. If not…" She trailed off, hating the idea of giving up on Celeste's life, but knowing this was a battle she might not win, after all. "If not, she'd be the first one to tell me I can't give in to someone like Tiberius in order to save her. The evil he brings to the world is too big for that. We can't weigh it against one life, no matter how much I want to."

He'd watched her intently while she spoke, and now nodded. "Okay."

She paused, waiting for more. "That's it? Just 'okay'?"

"You want a marching band?" But he leaned in, and touched his lips to hers. "I'm sorry," he whispered against her mouth. "I won't assume the worst of you again."

She leaned into his warmth and whispered in return, "Thank you."

They stayed like that for a moment, each drawing strength from the other. Then she drew back. "What happens now?"

He looked her in the eye and said, "Within the next two days, my team and a few handpicked combat veterans are going to raid the island in an effort to prevent Tiberius from selling the bug to four very nasty people who are in the middle of four different trials with pivotal DNA evidence."

She appreciated that he'd trusted her with the information so soon after their tentative truce. But she frowned when the information didn't quite line up. "If the trials are already in progress, they've already got the DNA evidence. Infecting the defendants won't change anything."

"It will if they also arrange to lose, destroy or otherwise taint the existing DNA samples, necessitating the drawing of new samples," he countered. "And trust me, they will."

She looked at him for a long moment. "You don't live in a very nice world, do you?"

He seemed surprised by the question, shrugged it off. "I'm used to the scumbags. They don't get to me anymore."

I think they do, she contradicted inwardly. *You just try very hard not to show it.* Iceman, indeed. It wasn't that he didn't feel the emotions, she was coming to realize. It was that he didn't know what to do with them, so he shoved them deep down inside and pretended they didn't exist.

But she didn't think he needed—or wanted—to hear that right now, so she said instead, "Be careful on the island. It's not a very nice place."

In fact, the thought of him going to Rocky Cliff chilled her to her very marrow. She wanted to tell him not to go, but she didn't have the right. It was his job. His duty.

And he wouldn't have had to go if it hadn't been for her stupidly arrogant decisions a year ago, she knew.

"I need you," he said unexpectedly, and for a moment she thought he was finished, that he was talking about the two of them. But then he said, "The team needs you. Anything else you can tell us about Rocky Cliff, we need to know it. Anything at all." When she didn't answer right away, he squeezed her hands. "Please, Sydney."

"Don't make me go back there." A whisper was all she could manage.

"No!" He nearly shouted the word. "Hell, no. You're strictly behind-the-scenes on this one. Intel only. Okay?"

"Yeah." She nodded. "Okay. When do we start?"

He stood, drawing her to her feet. "We just did."

Chapter Nine

Twenty hours later, Sydney was back on the north shore of Massachusetts, where it all began.

The team stayed in a large chain hotel farther down the coast rather than the quaint Gloucester B and B she'd used the last night before she'd departed for Rocky Cliff Island a year earlier, but that difference hardly mattered.

She leaned on the railing of the small, beach-facing deck that opened off her room and sighed, feeling as though she was right back where she'd started.

The ocean stretched to the horizon, where gray water met gray sky. It was chilly and faintly damp, and the beach was deserted save for a young man throwing a tennis ball for a wet, sand-covered black dog. In the adjoining rooms on either side of hers, Sharpe and his teammates were nailing down last-minute details. Knowing it, she should've felt surrounded and protected.

Instead, she felt very alone, just as she'd felt the last time she'd been here.

Then, as now, she wasn't sure what the future was

going to hold for her. Then, as now, she was making decisions she wasn't sure were right.

A year ago, she'd been working to convince herself that the ends justified the means, that it was okay to work for a man like Tiberius if the final results would benefit the greater good. Boy, she'd been seriously wrong about that one. And that made her question whether she was doing things wrong again this time.

Sure, it was Sharpe's plan, and it would be his decision to pull the trigger and launch the raid on the island the following day, but the entire strategy was based on her inside knowledge of the compound and the guards. What if she'd gotten it wrong? What if she'd forgotten something or remembered something wrong?

What if Tiberius captured them?

The past few days hadn't been the best of times by any means, but she'd grown fond of each member of Sharpe's team. Jimmy might be a self-proclaimed computer nerd, but he had a wickedly quirky sense of humor and a girlfriend named Sue. Drew, who'd worked with her on the maps and schematics, had made her feel like part of the team rather than an outsider. Megan, new and slightly shy, brought in to cover Grace's spot, had a dolphin's smile that tipped up at the corners and made Sydney want to smile in return. Sydney had spent the least amount of time with Michael, but he made her think of military recruiting posters, America and apple pie. She had a feeling it would be tough to feel unsafe around him. And Sharpe…

Well, Sharpe was Sharpe. On the up side, he smiled at her in passing. On the down side, she had no idea what that meant.

His mistrust was so deeply ingrained, she wasn't sure she could rely on him to believe her when it truly mattered. So why did her body come to life when he walked into the room, even though they hadn't kissed—hadn't so much as touched—since that night at his place?

And why, in the deepest darkness of the night, when she awoke from terrible, torturous dreams so vivid she could hear Jenny Marie's screams ringing in her ears, did she find herself holding his face in the forefront of her mind as she tried to soothe herself back to sleep?

The "why" is obvious, she told herself as she stood on the hotel deck and stared out over the ocean, which was darkening with the early spring dusk and the threat of an incoming storm. *The question is, what are you going to do about it?*

The smart answer was "nothing."

Then again, she was one of the dumbest smart people she knew.

"See something out there?" a deep, masculine voice said from behind her. She didn't need the fine shimmer of nerves and heat to tell her it was Sharpe.

She shook her head, not looking at him. "Just thinking."

"Must not be very good thoughts. You were frowning." He moved up beside her, leaned his forearms on the deck railing in a position that mirrored her own and stared out across the water.

Their forearms barely brushed, but the light contact sent liquid fire through her veins.

"Do you blame me?" She figured that was a neutral enough response. Let him interpret it however he wanted.

"Of the two of us, I'd say I have more of a reason to be uneasy. I'm the one going to the island tomorrow."

"I know," she said softly. "I wish you weren't."

"It's part of the job."

"I'll worry."

He slanted her a look. "I should tell you not to."

"Are you?"

"No." He shifted closer, so they were touching at hip and shoulder as they both leaned on the railing, staring off across the sea, which was growing choppy with the turbulence of an incoming spring squall. "Partly because you'll do what you want regardless of what I say, and partly because I think I like the idea of you being back here, thinking about me."

"I will," she said softly.

The question that loomed unspoken between them was what sort of relationship would they have when he went? It would be easy to say they were friends of a sort, with the promise of so much more, but the kindling heat inside her, and the pressure of grief and fear in her chest, warned that it wouldn't be enough for her. She wanted more. She wanted him.

When he left the next day, she wanted him to take a piece of her along, not because she wanted to go to Rocky Cliff, but because she wanted him to come back safe. If she hadn't been escaping toward Celeste, she never would've made it off the island. Was it silly to think the same might work for him, that maybe he'd be a little more careful if he was coming back to something other than the job?

They hadn't settled anything between them, not

really. He'd promised to trust her, but that trust hadn't yet been tested. She'd promised to be on his side, but that hadn't been proven, either.

Still, they might not have another night. They had tonight.

She held out her hand. "Come inside."

He took her fingers in his but stayed put, looking down into her eyes. "Are you sure?"

There was no need to discuss what the invitation meant. The need for sex, the promise of it, spun out in the air separating them.

"I'm sure," she said, and willed him to see the truth in her eyes, willed him to believe her. "I don't want to wake up alone tomorrow."

They both knew what she was really saying was, *If you don't come back from the island, I don't want us to have missed this chance.* She didn't know if it'd last past tonight, didn't know if either of them was ready for it to continue onward. She did know, however, that she didn't want to live with the regret of not having taken this one night together with him.

She wanted him to have something to come back to, even if it was an illusion that dissipated once the danger was past.

"Come inside," she said again. "Please." As if in answer, the wind picked up, blowing between them, around them, and bringing the scent of the sea.

He lifted their joined hands. "Are you trying to save me, Sydney?"

Her laugh caught in her throat. "You're not a lost cause yet."

"That, sweetheart, is a matter of opinion." He closed the distance between them, and kissed her, and that was when she knew for certain. She wasn't in danger of falling for him.

She'd already fallen. She just hadn't hit bottom yet.

JOHN DIDN'T EVEN BOTHER trying to talk himself out of following her into her hotel room—he'd passed the point of no return. Hell, maybe he'd passed it days ago, while he'd sat on his own couch and watched her sleep.

Then, as now, fierce protectiveness welled up inside him. All-consuming possessiveness. She was his in a way he'd never known before, never wanted before. But now it was all about want as he slid the glass doors closed, shutting out the night. Shutting out the storm that had come in so quickly, and now announced its arrival with a sharp splatter of rain against the glass slider.

Knowing that the others were out but not how long they'd be gone, he locked the connecting doors to the rooms on either side of Sydney's. Then he turned to her, their hands still linked, and lifted his free hand to touch the ends of her dark hair and trace the soft curve of her cheek.

Her luscious brown eyes were shadowed and wary, and as fierce as they had been the first moment he saw her, dripping wet and spitting mad as she crouched on the deck of the coast guard cutter *Valiant,* ready to fight the world. Yet at the same time he saw a layer of vulnerability beneath. She was afraid for him, cared for him, and the knowledge resonated. It mattered, probably more than it should.

He needed to be focused when he led his team to the island the next day. He needed to be in charge, needed to be the Iceman, but that man seemed very far away as he leaned in and touched his lips to hers, and the layers of defense were stripped away, leaving only the man behind.

THE MOMENT THEIR lips touched, Sydney felt a shudder run through his big frame, as though something was changing within him. Then he slanted his mouth across hers and applied gentle suction, teasing her lips apart. His tongue touched hers, softly at first, and then with increasing pressure, and she knew she had him. He'd made his choice, and he'd chosen her.

Reveling in the knowledge, glorying in it, she lost herself in the kiss.

Fisting her hands in the fine cotton of his shirt, she leaned in and opened to him. Heat exploded inside her, muting the buzz of nerves at the thought that she was doing this, really doing this. With Sharpe. Or rather, *John.*

He pulled away and looked down at her. "What?"

She flushed when she realized she'd said it aloud. "I was practicing your name. It seems silly to think of you as Sharpe now."

"You can call me whatever feels right," he said simply, and the open invitation from a man as guarded as he was meant far more than it should have, sending a spear of emotion through her to join the heat.

She swallowed hard against the lure of affection— or more—and tried to keep it light, saying, "I'm all about doing what feels right."

Shifting her grip to the lapels of his suit jacket—navy today—she drew him down for another kiss, one that started with their lips curved in pleasure and quickly morphed to an openmouthed, searching exploration that detonated bombs of sensation in her fingertips, in her core, in all the neurons between.

Murmuring something—maybe appreciation, maybe a suggestion—he slid his hands up her ribs, skimming the outsides of her breasts and causing her nipples to tighten with anticipation.

She lit up, humming with the electricity that had flared between them from the first. Her mouth turned greedy, and she tugged the tails of his shirt from his waistband and ran her hands beneath. His stomach was warm and hard beneath her fingertips, dusted with the faint irregularity of masculine hair, and though he wasn't a bulky man by any means, everywhere she touched she found muscles that coiled in hard, ready knots beneath her hands.

Sliding her fingertips higher, playing across the hard ridges of muscle and man, she found her exploration blocked by the straps of his shoulder holster, so she reversed course, stroking down along his ribs to bracket his hips with her hands, then reaching up to tug at the holster. "You're going to need to lose this."

"I was just thinking the same thing." He stepped away from her, unhooked the holster and shrugged out of it as raindrops blew in from the sea and hit the sliding glass doors with the hard rat-tat of a spring storm.

Placing the holstered gun on the dresser top, beside the hotel-standard entertainment center, he clicked off the wall lamp, plunging the room into darkness. Then he crossed to her and urged her to the glass doors, pressing her against him and wrapping his arms around her so they were aligned back-to-front, both watching the night.

He grazed his lips across one of her ears, sending a shimmery sensation straight to her core, and whispered, "Listen to the storm."

The wild fury of it raged inland, whipping the waves to frenzied whitecaps that hurled themselves onward, only to die on the beach. The wind howled off the Atlantic, rattling the windows and making the glass bow in its frame. But Sydney felt safe in John's arms. Protected. Like they were cocooned together in a moment outside of normal time, where nothing and no one could touch them.

It was an illusion, she knew, brought by the night and the storm and the feelings that bound them together.

The danger was still out there, waiting.

For tonight, though, she was safe with him.

"Will the storm change your plans if it keeps up?" she said softly, not sure what she wanted the answer to be. Part of her wanted him to say yes, for them to have another day. But that would only prolong the inevitable.

"It'll pass," he said with quiet assurance. "We'll sneak onto the island tomorrow, as planned."

They had the loan of a boat bristling with the newest in stealth technology. The Renfrew brothers, along with a half dozen coast guarders and combat-trained men, would move in on the main dock as a distraction, allowing John's team to make it to one of the less patrolled beaches of Rocky Cliff Island. That was the theory, anyway.

In reality, so many things could go wrong, it made Sydney sick to think of the possibilities. So she let the storm beat in her blood, in her heart, and she turned in John's arms, leaned up on her tiptoes and pressed her lips to his.

Finally, she eased back and said, "Then let's not waste the hours we have left."

One corner of his mouth kicked up and his eyes turned sad, as though he'd read more into her words than she'd intended, but he said nothing, simply leaned down and kissed her. Then, without breaking the kiss, he swept her up into his arms and carried her the few steps to the bed.

The mattress yielded beneath their combined weight, and she gloried in the solidness of him pressing her down as she wrapped her legs around his, hooked her arms around his strong shoulders and gave herself up to the moment, to the spring storm, to the man.

Their kisses grew hotter and harder as the wind slapped stinging pellets of water against the glass barrier that was the only thing separating them from the maelstrom outside. The air in the small room heated with passion, with the mingling of their scents and the torturous rub of far too much clothing.

Sydney helped him wrestle her clinging pullover off over her head, then fumbled with the buttons on his shirt, parting the material so they could press skin-to-skin.

Far from being icy, he burned from within, his passion radiating outward and scorching her. She writhed beneath him as the heat built from want to an all-consuming need, until not even the storm mattered

anymore, until the only thing that mattered was him—
the taste of him, the good, solid weight of him and the
feel of his skin against hers.

Then even that wasn't enough anymore. She parted
her legs and slid her calves up his thighs on either side,
opening herself to the press of his solid length as he
began to rock against her.

Heat spiraled upward, breaking over them both until
he pulled away, breath rasping in his lungs. He held
himself there for a second, muscles so tight he was practically shaking, and in the darkness she felt him fight to
master himself, to stay in control.

The thought that she could bring a man like him to the
breaking point was brutally erotic, and she would have
slid against him, trying to drive him beyond. But then he
bent his head and touched his tongue to one of her peaked
nipples, suckling her through the fabric of her bra, and
all other thoughts were lost in a wave of sensation.

She arched up beneath him and cried out. Dimly
aware of the people who might or might not be in the
rooms on either side, she clamped her lips together,
stifling further cries as he drove her up using only his
lips on her breasts. His clever fingers trailed along her
body, touching her. Inciting her. Promising dark
delights. Teasing her beyond reason.

She pushed his unbuttoned shirt off over his shoulders, laughing when it snagged on his wrists and he
reared up to yank it free. By unspoken accord they rolled
apart and pulled off the rest of their clothes, with him
pausing a moment to slip a condom from his billfold.

She didn't ask how long it had been there or who it'd

been intended for. She was only grateful he had one, because if they'd been forced to stop now, she might've screamed in frustration.

The need for sex, the glory of it, beat hammer-loud in her blood, and sang in her ears, drowning out the fury of the storm outside.

Once he had the condom in place she reached for him, drew him down and offered herself to him, demanded he come to her and welcomed him when he did. It had been so long for her that she was tight, bringing a moment of pain as he entered her, followed by the burn of pleasure, the gut-wrenching feeling of being full, of being joined.

Of being connected. To him. Only to him.

Once he was fully seated with her, he paused and dropped his brow to hers for a second as they breathed in tandem, absorbing the moment, the sensation. An unexpectedly poignant ache fisted in her chest, just beneath her heart, and she closed her eyes tightly against the promise of tears.

If this was it for them, she thought, it would have to be enough.

Then he began to move within her, and the sadness gave way to a roar of heat and need, and the delicious, wonderful friction they created together. The mad power of it broke over them like one of the storm-tossed waves, but instead of cresting and losing momentum it kept building, kept driving them up until they were racing to the peak, gasping and hanging on to each other while he drove into her and she clung to him.

And when they got there, she turned her face into the pillow to muffle her cries of completion, and he shuddered and groaned close to her ear, keeping the moment private, keeping it hidden from the others.

Afterward, she wrapped herself around him, turned her face into his throat and clung to him some more while the world changed shape around her, and she thought, *This is it. This is what it feels like to love a man.*

At one point she'd thought she'd loved Richard, but she'd long ago realized she'd loved the idea of him far more than the reality, had loved the symmetry of being with someone from within the small world of the university. In the end, it hadn't even been much of a surprise to learn that he'd stolen some of her work and claimed it as his own, then ran to the dean's committee and accused her before she could accuse him.

It had been messy and embarrassing, but it hadn't been heartache, not really.

Not the way she felt it as she slid toward sleep, knowing that when the dawn broke, the man she loved would be going up against a monster.

HOURS LATER, Sydney awoke to the shrill ring of a strange phone. Groaning, she rolled over and fumbled for the thing, blearily registering the hotel room and a scattering of her belongings, and snapping to attention when she saw unfamiliar clothes slung over the desk chair—suit pants and a button-down shirt—and a holster neatly folded on the desk.

The sight made her acutely aware of the warmth at her back, and the rumble of a man's breath.

She'd slept with Sharpe. With *John*. He'd stayed the night.

Consciousness returned with a punch of heat, and the memory of them turning to each other time and again through the night, each encounter growing slower and more languid, though no less hot. More like affection than flat-out lust. Almost, at times, bordering on more. Almost like love.

Don't even go there, she warned herself, glancing over at him and stilling at the sight of him sprawled on his stomach, gloriously naked and gloriously male, with his face jammed under his pillow as if to keep the morning away a few moments longer.

Fully appreciating the desire and knowing they damn well needed to keep their night a secret from the others, lest it disrupt the day's plan, she kept her voice low when she answered, "Hello?"

She expected one of Sharpe's teammates or maybe the front desk.

She got a smooth, silky voice that was all too familiar.

"Rise and shine, Sydney." Tiberius couldn't have sounded more charming, as if he was holding all the cards in the deck at once. "But don't—" he emphasized the word with a snarl "—even think of waking Agent Sharpe. If you look to your left, you'll see why."

Fear seized her by the throat, closing off her breath, choking her until the world spun. Shaking, afraid to look and afraid not to look, she turned her head.

The green dot of a laser-guided gun sight danced across the back of Sharpe's neck, skittered along his dark, thick hair and slid to his temple.

"Boom," Tiberius said in her ear. "That's what'll happen if you don't cooperate. Nod if you understand."

She nodded as a tear slid down her cheek and sobs backed up in her throat.

"Good girl. I want you to get up and get dressed. There's a car waiting for you outside. Do you understand?"

Another nod.

"You have two minutes. And Sydney?"

He waited for a response, forcing her to whisper, "Yes?"

"The sniper will remain in place until you're on one of my boats, headed for Rocky Cliff Island. If you do anything—and I mean anything—to signal Sharpe or the other members of his team, then he's dead. They're all dead…and they won't enjoy it."

He hung up before she could nod, but the green light shifted, crawling across Sharpe's arm and up her thigh, pausing a second to circle the area of her breasts, which were hidden by the sheet she clutched to her chest.

She batted at the light, trying to shoo it away as tears blurred her vision.

Then the green dot moved to the alarm clock as if to say, *Ten minutes, Sydney. Don't be late, or he's dead.*

She hit the ground running and told herself not to look back.

THE MORNING OF the mission to Tiberius's island, the Iceman overslept. He didn't wake up until his cell phone went off with the raucous shrill he'd programmed in on the theory that only the dead could sleep through something that loud.

Even then, it was a struggle.

He felt heavy-limbed and lethargic, as if he'd been drugged or beaten up, or had a night of really great—

Sex. Oh, hell.

Shooting upright in bed, he grabbed for his cell phone. A second before he answered, he got a good look around and realized he wasn't in his room. He dropped the phone when he realized he was in Sydney's room, and odds were that his entire team knew it.

He could trust them to keep that quiet from the higher-ups, but that wasn't the point. They knew. And in a couple of hours, he was going to be leading them on a hell of a dangerous insertion, based on information they'd gotten from Sydney. From his lover.

The thought brought a wash of heat and an ache of tenderness in the region of his heart, one that he thought he might be able to get used to over time. Despite their problems and differences, she was exactly the sort of woman he wanted at his side—clever and resourceful, tough enough to stand up to him when he got off track, tender enough to let him be tender in return.

He scratched his bare chest in the region of that ache as his phone chimed again.

"Better get dressed," he called in the direction of the bathroom. "We're about to have company, and they're not going to be happy."

Maybe the sex had dazed him or maybe he was just an idiot, because he actually expected an answer.

He didn't get one.

His stomach hit the deck in zero seconds flat. A quick look confirmed that her clothes and shoes were gone, and he knew better than to think she'd up and gone for a walk when her life was in danger.

He'd been played. Again.

Damn it.

Snapping the rest of the way awake, he erupted from the bed and yanked on his clothes, simultaneously barking into the phone, "Meet me in the spare room in sixty seconds. We've got a problem."

He hung up the phone, strapped on his holster and strode to the door.

He left his jacket behind because suits were for civilized people, and he was done being civilized.

The team was already assembled in the spare room when he got there, and from the looks of their take-out coffee cups they'd been there for a while already. He met their stares, owning every skin-crawling second of embarrassment. "I slept with her and she took off while I was zonked out. The last time I looked at the clock was four hours ago, so we can assume she's already on the island and the mission is FUBARed. Any questions?"

Michael frowned and looked at Jimmy. "Are you sure she didn't leave under duress? We could check the hotel switchboard. Maybe Tiberius called and threatened her or something."

"What's left for him to threaten?" John snapped. "We've got Celeste under wraps, and Sydney doesn't have any other close ties." At the sidelong looks, he growled, "What, she played you guys, too? Trust me, we're a means to an end, not close ties."

For a second he remembered the night before, when she'd whispered love words to him—not the big three, but endearments laced with soft, womanly affection. Acid burned his gut when he accepted that as nothing more than setting the groundwork for today.

He clenched his teeth and gritted. "I want everyone ready to roll in thirty minutes, as planned."

Jimmy frowned. "He's expecting us."

"Exactly." John nodded sharply. "We're going to use that against him and take the whole damn island with us."

"What about Sydney?" Michael persisted. "If she's there under duress, if she's innocent—"

"She's not innocent," John snapped. "Trust me on that one. And if she gets hurt, then that's no more than she deserves for serving a master like Tiberius."

His voice was harsh, his mien harsher, but as he turned away and strode from the room, grief, guilt and anger pinched beneath his heart.

He'd liked the woman she'd pretended to be, damn it. Maybe could've even loved her.

In reality, though, Sydney was no better than Rose: both traitors.

Chapter Ten

The island looks exactly the same, Sydney thought dully as the motorboat approached the pier.

Then again, she'd only been gone a week. She was the one who'd changed. She'd escaped and she'd gotten her sister to safety as planned. But she'd also gotten involved with a man and a cause, and that hadn't been part of the plan at all.

She'd left Rocky Cliff Island looking for a way to save her own ass. She was returning in order to make things right. Or so she kept telling herself. She had a feeling John would see it far differently. He'd promised to believe her, promised to trust her, but how could a man like him trust her in the face of overwhelming evidence to the contrary?

The fact was that when Tiberius called, she'd come running. That was all John would see, she was sure of it.

Tears filled Sydney's eyes as the boat bumped up against the dock, but she sniffed and brushed them away. This was her choice, her responsibility. She'd been a coward before, hiding behind Celeste's illness, using it as an excuse to make the choices she knew in her gut weren't right. But not anymore.

This time, she was doing what was right; she was going to undo what she never should've done in the first place.

And then Tiberius was going to kill her.

"Off," one of the guards said, and shoved her toward the dock. There were three guards on the boat, all heavily armed. They stayed stone-faced as they marched her up the ramp leading from the dock to the mansion.

Tiberius's grand house sat on the crest of the island's single large hill. The land rose up through the levels of security, past guard shacks, cameras and patrols to the main house, and then fell away on the other side in a sheer drop of several hundred feet, providing the cliffs that gave the island its name.

The sun shone on the scene with false cheer, but otherwise everything was the same as it had been when she'd escaped. The guard shacks didn't look any different, the buildings were all placed where she'd put them on the map she and Jimmy had built together. From the movements of the patrols they passed on their way up to the house, she was pretty sure they were on patrol rotation B that day.

All of which meant absolutely nothing under the current circumstances.

They entered the mansion through the front door rather than the side exit she'd escaped through.

The house was a sprawling affair originally designed in the style of the old Newport mansions, with twelve-foot ceilings and exquisitely carved moldings. The main foyer was twice that high and led to a master staircase made of pink-veined marble and granite. Instead of looking grand and lush, though, the place seemed sterile. There was no artwork on the walls, no sense that it was anything but a place of business, as evidenced by the security cameras in the corners, constantly scanning the scene, and the sense of purposeful motion elsewhere in the house.

Sydney automatically turned right, toward the lab and her quarters, but one of the guards grabbed her arm and redirected her toward the big marble staircase. "Not the lab. You're going upstairs."

The directive chilled her to her bones, proving that she wasn't nearly as calm or as brave as she wanted to think.

Prodded by the guards, she mounted the stairs. Instead of turning toward the security hub, though, they herded her down a long hall that ran at a tangent to a wing she hadn't been in before.

Nerves closed in, nearly choking her and forcing the question from between her trembling lips. "Where are you taking me?"

The guards didn't answer as they stopped her in front of a grandly carved set of twelve-foot-high double doors, inset with a normal-size door. One of the men knocked, then turned the knob and opened the normal-size door. The other two guards hustled her inside.

The room was a huge salon done in reds and golds, with lush-looking draperies and tapestries. A small dining table for four sat in one corner near a set of ornate French doors, and in the center of the room sat a claw-footed mahogany suite of sofa, chairs, end tables and a low coffee table. Several doors led from the room, all of them closed.

Unlike the rest of the mansion, the salon contained personal touches, including soft landscapes on the walls, and a man's jacket tossed over one of the chairs.

Sydney's breath froze in her lungs. She didn't need to see into the other rooms to figure out where they'd brought her. The place fit Jenny Marie's description to a T.

She was in Tiberius's personal quarters.

But why?

The guards shoved her into one of the claw-footed chairs, turned on their heels and left. The moment the hallway door shut behind them, one of the far doorways swung open and Tiberius stepped through.

Tall and gaunt, with thinning gray hair and a Trump-like comb-over, wearing a dull gray suit that hung on his frame, he looked like a college professor, or maybe a mortician. Not a master criminal. Not a killer.

Yet he was both of those things, and so many more, none of them good.

Heart pounding, Sydney stood and faced him, trying not to show her fear even though she was so terrified her mouth had gone dry and her knees shook.

He didn't even bother to gloat, merely crossed the room and pressed some sort of mechanism. A panel slid aside in the wall and a hardwired computer station moved into view. "Give me the password."

She lifted her chin with false bravery. "No."

He smiled without humor. "You like deals, don't you? How about this one—you give me the correct password and unlock the computers. Once I've downloaded the sequence and pulled the samples from the freezers you

so cleverly locked tight, we'll leave the island together."
He paused and a mad glint entered his eyes. "If you try
anything funny, though, like keying in the wrong word,
I'll still be leaving, but you'll be stuck here, on this
chunk of rock…which is set to blow in—" he checked
his watch "—thirty-eight minutes and change. It's not
as fitting an end as I would've liked, but the result is the
same. Boom!" He made an exploding motion with his
hands. He mocked a frown. "Oh, and I'm sorry about
your boyfriend, by the way." At her baffled look, he
smiled. "Didn't you know? He and his teammates are
trying to sneak onto the backside of the island as we
speak. They should be getting here just in time to watch
us take off. That is, if you're as smart as I think you are."

"No." At first there was no volume to the word, so
Sydney tried again. "No deal."

"What, you want better terms?" He smirked. "Don't
even think I'm giving you Sharpe. It's your life for the
password, take it or leave it."

A year ago, maybe even a few weeks ago, she might
have been tempted, might have convinced herself it was
better to live and fight another day. But meeting John
Sharpe—caring for him—had changed all that, because
he was a man who fought every fight, every time. And
if she was on his team, could she do any less?

"I'm waiting." Tiberius crossed his arms. "The password, please."

Sydney bowed her head in submission and crossed
to the computer terminal. She touched the back of the
desk chair with shaking fingers, pulling it out of the
knee hole so she could sit.

Then, before she could wimp out, she snatched up the chair and threw it at Tiberius. He shouted and batted it aside as she broke for the French doors, one of which was cracked open, leading out onto a carved marble veranda with a delicate wrought-iron railing.

Sydney's heartbeat hammered in her ears.

Footsteps rang out behind her, along with the sound of slamming doors and Tiberius's shout of "Get her!"

The guards opened fire. As the first bullets whizzed past and slapped into the doorway, sending up chips of wood and marble, Sydney didn't think.

Screaming, she grabbed on to the railing, swung up and over and let go, flinging herself off the second floor balcony.

Mercifully the land sloped up beneath the house, so the fall was manageable. She landed in a beach plum bush and cried out when the thorns bit into her skin. Rolling away, she struggled to her feet and started running, heading along the side of the house, along one of the faint tracks she'd found on her guided walks during her captivity.

There were shouts from up above. Worse, she could hear one of the outdoor patrols closing in on her from the side.

Breath whistling in her lungs, she bolted for the cliff.

And prayed she'd find her team in time.

JOHN WAS ABLE TO INSERT his team exactly as planned. The distraction team around the front of the island made a big, loud raid on the docks, and let themselves be repelled after a good ten minutes of gunplay. Under that cover, John, Jimmy, Michael and Drew slipped their stealth-cloaked boat into the landing spot they'd chosen.

Located a solid mile from the main compound, with twenty-foot-high rock ledges on either side of the tiny beach, the landing spot was less than ideal. In fact, it had been on the bottom of the list Sydney had come up with for possible drop points…which was why he'd chosen it.

After her disappearance, there was no way he was using one of her top choices. He still couldn't believe she'd left, couldn't believe she'd gone to the island. But surveillance cameras near the Gloucester marina had shown her climbing out of a car under heavy guard, and getting into one of Tiberius's boats.

Granted, the armed guards suggested she'd been taken under duress, and a check of incoming calls to the hotel confirmed Michael's suggestion that she'd received a call from the island, but that hardly mattered to John. She'd chosen to give in to Tiberius's pressure rather than waking him, rather than trusting him to protect her, and that galled him beyond words.

"We're going in," Michael called from the helm. "Hang on, it's going to be rough!"

The tide was on its way out, creating swirling riptides that threatened to suck the boat into the nearby cliffs, slam it into the rocks and end the attack before it even began.

Michael fought the controls with grim determination, legs set wide apart for balance, cursing under his breath and babying the powerful engine as he fought the swirling pull of water. Drew had strapped himself into one of the pilot's chairs and was backing Michael up wherever possible. Jimmy was hanging on to a sideways-facing seat, looking decidedly green. John sat facing forward, braced against the swell, his jaw locked.

He didn't feel sick, didn't feel scared. He felt…numb.

There could be no future where there wasn't any trust, and though he'd fought the realization as long and as hard as he could, Sydney's actions that morning only proved what he'd suspected from the very beginning: she had her own agenda, and wasn't above twisting the rules to suit her needs.

She might've told herself she was giving in to save him or some such nonsense, but in the end it came down to not trusting him enough to do his job, not trusting him to keep the two of them alive.

Damn her, he thought, raw hurt expanding in his chest. Why hadn't she just woken him up?

He saw Drew glance back, and though he couldn't hear the other man's words over the crashing surf and the laboring whine of the boat's engines, he read his lips as he said to Michael, "Sharpe's looking cool. We'll be okay."

I'm not cool, he wanted to say, *I'm numb.*

But because he knew his team needed him to be strong, he unstrapped himself from his chair and took up position directly behind Michael and Drew, hanging on to the back of the two captain's chairs and riding the heaving deck on braced legs. "Looking good," he said. "We're almost there."

The small gravel strip was no more than fifty feet away, but there was a vicious whip of crosscurrent in the gap, and the intersection of the riptide with the crosscurrent created an area of man-high chop. The cliffs bounced the sea breeze around, creating nearly gale-force winds in that small area, even though the day beyond was bright and sunny.

The comm device inside John's raincoat crackled with Dick Renfrew's voice reporting that they were pulling back to wait for further instructions, and god-speed to the island team.

It was time to do or die.

"Hang on!" Michael yelled, the wind whipping the words away the moment they were out of his mouth. "We're going in!"

He kicked the engines full-throttle, aiming upstream of the current in the hopes that by the time they were through, they'd be on dry land.

Or splintered against the rocks. One or the other.

John hooked his feet beneath the ankle rests of each pilot's chair and tightened his grip as the boat surged forward with a howl, leaped up the side of a wave and hung there, poised motionless for a moment, before crashing into the trough and burying its nose in the sea.

At a moment when he should've been on an adrenaline high, should've been bracing for a crash, or prepping for the fight to come, he was wishing he were somewhere else. Wishing he were some*one* else.

Suddenly, he was beyond weary of the job.

Why bother? There was always another criminal looking to wreak havoc. Every time he and his team took one down, another sprang up to fill the vacuum created. What would really happen if they all simply quit one day? Would the terrorist community eventually reach some sort of equilibrium?

You're losing it, John told himself. *Get your head back in the game.*

He needed a vacation, he thought incongruously, hanging on to the seats as a ten-foot whitecap hit them broadside, nearly turtling the twenty-foot craft. Michael and Drew fought the controls, forcing the boat to churn through the white spume. Jimmy had gone from green to gray and looked like he was praying.

Meanwhile, John was realizing there was really no place he wanted to go. For that matter, what would he do if he up and left the Bureau? Sure, it might be fun to tinker with the house for a few months, but then what? He didn't have anything else. Didn't have anything but the job.

And damn Sydney again for bringing that painfully home inside him.

Even as he despaired in his soul, his brain stayed cool, scanning the scene and calculating options. He saw the gap and pointed. "There!"

Michael nodded and aimed the floundering boat through the patch of incongruously glass-smooth water. Like a biker skimming across hardpan after laboring through beach sand, the boat shot forward, gaining momentum enough to slew through the last section of water and fling itself up the beach with a sideways, jolting slide.

"Let's go!" Drew took a flying leap off the boat and grabbed the towline off the front. Jimmy wasn't far behind him, moving fast on shaky legs. The two quickly started looking for a stone outcropping to tie off to, or failing that, a crevice they could set an eyebolt into.

Michael stayed on board, manning the controls in case a larger wave slapped onto the beach and threatened to float the craft off. He called, "Get the line as high as you can, so the boat can move with the tide if necessary."

Don't bother, John almost said. *We won't need it past tide change.*

The way he saw it, by that time either they would've already captured the island or they'd be dead. He didn't see a viable option that involved retreat.

But he also knew that wasn't the Iceman speaking, it was someone else entirely, someone who ran on emotion rather than logic. Someone whose heart hurt in his chest. Someone who would do them no good on the mission ahead.

Focus, he told himself. *Forget the woman. Find the game.*

"We're good," Jimmy called, and tossed down the line. Once the boat was tied fast, John distributed their packs, which were loaded with the weapons and other gear they'd projected needing for the op.

By the time he'd jumped down off the boat and shouldered his own pack, he'd more or less found the calm that'd served him so well throughout his life. The moment his boots hit the gravel, signaling that it was time to roll, the questions and regrets that'd plagued him on the boat ceased to exist, or if they existed, they'd been shoved so far down into his psyche that they wouldn't interfere.

He was in the zone. Game on.

After reporting their position to the other boat in a brief burst of radio traffic—they were using a scrambled channel but still keeping the chatter to a minimum—John led his men toward the likeliest-seeming trail up the cliff face.

"There's more of an angle than I expected," he said, as much to himself as to the others. "We may not even need the ropes."

"First good news we've had all day," Drew muttered, and John couldn't disagree.

Still, it took them a few minutes to work their way up to the top of the cliff, testing their way and setting ropes as necessary. When they reached the edge, John used an angled mirror on a telescoping handle—an old technology, but smaller and lighter than the newer fiber-optic units, and fine for basic sneak-a-peek stuff—to check out what was going on above them.

"All clear," he mouthed to Drew, who was directly behind him, followed by Jimmy, with Michael taking the rear point position.

John slipped up and over the rocky lip, onto a flat promontory that was nothing but windswept rock for the first fifteen feet or so before giving way to a tangle of salt-stunted evergreens and low island scrub.

Seeing no signs of resistance, he beckoned the others up and over. As planned, they set eyehooks and climbing ropes near the edge, in case they needed a quick exit. Once that was done, they slipped into the forest of stunted evergreens, walking single file and keeping a sharp watch for hostile company.

Jimmy tracked their course and progress on a hand-held GPS unit. They were still a half mile away from the main compound when John heard a noise coming from up ahead.

Senses alert, he stopped and gestured for the others to fade into the surrounding trees.

He strained to pinpoint the noise. He'd thought… there! He pointed off to the east, where a thicker stand of taller trees shaded the landscape. Michael nodded. He'd heard the footsteps, too. Moving silently, the marksman readied his weapon, knowing they couldn't let an alarm get back to the main compound.

Not yet, anyway.

The sounds grew louder as the guard approached, making straight for Michael's position and moving fast.

John's heart rate increased at the thought that they'd already been discovered, but he didn't move or make a sound to indicate the suspicion, instead tensing as the noises angled away, then looped around suddenly, headed straight for his position.

Without time to pull his own weapon, and afraid that the screening trees nearby would foul Michael's shot, John didn't stop to think.

He acted.

Lunging out of his scrubby concealment, he caught the guard in a flying tackle, clapping a hand across the bastard's mouth and slamming him to the ground.

Working on icy logic and instinct rather than the mores of civilization, he had his combat knife out and was a heartbeat away from the guard's throat when he realized two things that had him pausing the final blow.

One, the guy wasn't big enough to be one of Tiberius's guards, and two, the guy wasn't a guy.

It was Sydney.

The realization flared through his gut in a burst of heat and anger that came straight from the place he'd locked away for the duration of the op. He spat a curse and rolled aside, rising to his feet before he turned back and looked down at her.

She was wearing the same clothes she'd had on the day—and night—before, and she had a faint bruise along her jaw. Her face and arms were scratched and bleeding, and she was breathing hard, as though she'd run all the way from the mansion. Her eyes were worried and scared and faintly defiant, as though she already knew what he was going to say, and didn't plan to back down.

Her eyes locked on his. "He said he was going to kill you if I didn't go with his people," she said, her voice low and rasping with the effort of her breaths. "At the hotel. There was a sniper outside the window. I saw the laser dot on your forehead."

"Don't expect me to thank you for saving my ass," John said coolly. "You should've woken me and let me do my damn job." He paused. "Did you give him the password?"

She met him stare for stare. "No, but there's something more. He's wired the island to blow. You've got maybe twenty-five minutes or so left on the countdown."

John's gut iced. "How do you know?"

"He told me."

"And then he just, what? Let you go?" He scoffed in disbelief.

"I went out the window." Her voice went low. "I'm telling you the truth."

Yeah, he thought, *but sometimes the truth isn't enough. Sometimes there's got to be trust, too.*

And that was something they apparently didn't have.

Unable to respond to her, unable to figure out how, he turned away from her, gesturing for the others to get her up. "She comes with us."

He heard her quiet sob as he walked away, but he didn't turn back. He'd already given her one too many chances.

Whether or not she was working for Tiberius, caring for her was a liability he couldn't afford right now. He had a job to do.

Chapter Eleven

Silent tears stung Sydney's eyes as she stumbled along in John's wake. She couldn't stop looking at him, at the tense set of his shoulders and the uncompromising line of his square jaw, couldn't stop remembering the night before, when she'd run her hands over those same broad shoulders and tasted the skin along that square jaw.

Though she hadn't gone to bed with him expecting a future, she'd hoped for more than the night. Then Tiberius had called. Damn him. And damn John for not trusting her enough to hear her out, for not caring enough to try to see her side of things.

The rising burn of anger dried her tears. Her legs ached from her flight from the mansion and trembled with the knowledge that she was headed back there yet again. She knew John would keep her as safe as possible—he had a core of honor, whether he trusted her or not—but she couldn't shake the terrible knowledge that none of this was going as planned.

Or rather, none of it was going according to their plan. She suspected they were playing right into Tiberius's hands, because now if he captured the team, he'd not only get another chance to strip the password from her, he'd also have the opportunity to rid himself of a major foe in Sharpe and his team.

Or he'd just take off and hope they blew up with the island, because it sure didn't seem like John had believed her on that front, either.

Run! she wanted to say. *Let's go, let's get out of here.* But she didn't, because he wasn't listening to her.

She could only trudge along behind him, wishing she'd done things differently, wishing that she'd never taken Tiberius's damn job in the first place, or that the messages she'd managed to sneak off the island had been to the authorities rather than to Celeste.

But wishing for something was never enough to make it happen. If that were the case, her parents would've returned when they were children, Celeste would be healed and John would've known instinctively how to trust her.

Unfortunately, it seemed like all the wishes in the world wouldn't be enough to make that happen.

"We're almost there," Jimmy whispered from behind her, his voice almost soundless.

John heard him, though, and brought the team to a halt. Michael covered Sydney—his expression apologetic—while the others had a quick confab. After a minute, John gestured to the sharpshooter. "You two stay here. We're going to split up, find someplace to stash her and do a quick recon. When I get back, you can—"

A crack of gunfire cut him off, the bullet splintering the tree to his immediate left.

In the next moment, all hell broke loose.

The teammates dove for cover while Sydney stared, slow to react from the shock of it all, the strangeness of what her life had come to.

"Get her down!" someone shouted, but the voice seemed to come from far away, muted beneath the chatter of gunfire.

"Damn it, Sydney, get *down!*" John hit her with a flying tackle, grabbing her by the waist and dragging them both to the ground.

Instead of landing flat atop her, he twisted them in midair so they landed on their sides facing each other, with his arms looped around her waist and their noses nearly touching. The hard metal of his gun pressed into her, but she barely noticed the discomfort. She was caught in his eyes, which blazed with fury and maybe something else. Something hotter and less certain, something that made her think that maybe he'd heard her, after all. Maybe a small part of him believed her.

He didn't speak, though. Instead, he scrambled to a low crouch and joined his teammates in returning fire.

But the counterattack was too little, too late. Sharpe's team was surrounded and outgunned. Within minutes, Tiberius's guards had overrun their position. They quickly disarmed the team members, stripped their gear away and secured them with zip ties.

They did Sharpe first, and they weren't gentle. Tears tracked down Sydney's cheeks as he stared at her.

She couldn't read his expression, but guilt had her blurting, "I didn't lead them to you. I didn't tell them anything."

He didn't get a chance to answer—even if he'd been

planning to—because the guards who'd tied him yanked him to his feet and prodded him with his rifle butt. "Shut up and move."

As the guards herded them to the main house, John and Sydney wound up walking near each other. He bent low so he could whisper in her ear, "I believe you, about that at least. I just wish you'd trusted me enough to let me take care of Tiberius. You shouldn't be here."

Tears stung Sydney's eyes. "I'm sorry. I—"

"Keep moving." The guards shoved her ahead of the others, and then when they reached the house, hustled her down the hallway to the right, away from the others. Ignoring her struggles and panicked shouts, they pushed her through the door to her old quarters and locked her in.

"John," she shouted. *"John!"* She didn't see where they'd taken the others, but feared she could guess.

Upstairs. To the security hub.

HE HEARD HER CALL his name, heard her voice break on the scream, and nearly tore into the guards in an effort to get to her, but he forced aside the emotions in favor of logic. Barely.

It wouldn't help if he got himself shot in the process of getting to her. He had to bide his time. Work with his team. Think it through.

The emotion had to exist alongside logic.

Somewhere along the line he'd started to realize that the things he was feeling for her didn't have to weaken him. Far from it. Caring for her made him stronger, made him want to tear into his foe to get to her, to protect her. He needed to temper the urge with rationality, though, or he'd start making mistakes.

The guards split the team up, with three armed men marching Michael, Jimmy and Drew in one direction, while two others prodded John through a doorway.

They locked the door behind him, and the clank of metal on metal sounded very loud. Very final.

He found himself in the security hub, a large room with one wall completely given over to a flat screen, on which a shifting array of televised images showed most of the island. A bank of desks faced the displays and held computer stations manned by more of the stone-faced guards.

The agent inside John, the one that had ruled his thoughts and actions for so many years, automatically cataloged the men and armaments in the room—six men, two with obvious weapons—and mapped out his options for escape…slim to none.

He was in the middle of cobbling together a desper-ate plan of attack when Tiberius stepped in through a door in the far wall, and the game changed.

Wearing a mustard-colored tweed jacket and darker corduroy pants, the self-proclaimed "opportunistic busi-nessman" looked even more like a college professor than he did in his file photos. Unlike so many of the criminals John had sought—and brought to justice—over the years, his eyes weren't dead or cold, or even angry. Instead, he carried a faintly amused, faintly down-trodden air that made him seem completely unre-markable.

That was one of the things that made him so incredibly dangerous, John knew. He appeared so trustworthy and nonthreatening on the surface. It was only when the layers started to peel back that the real evil became apparent, and by then, it was usually too late for the innocent victim to escape.

And despite the gray areas she'd strayed into, Sydney was one of them. An innocent. The blood of the dead wasn't on her hands, John finally acknowledged to himself when he'd put the guilt on her for far too long.

The dead belonged entirely to Tiberius and his peculiar brand of mad genius.

Tiberius stayed halfway across the room, keeping the guards between John and himself, and gave the agent a good, long look. "I don't have time to waste with power plays and negotiations, Agent Sharpe, so here's the deal. You get your girlfriend to turn over the password, and you two and the rest of your team are free to get back in your not-so-stealthy boat and head back to the mainland ahead of the blast that I'm sure dear Sydney told you about."

What makes you think she'd do anything I ask? John wanted to say, because she was nothing if not headstrong…which was one of the things he respected about her.

No, damn it. It was one of the things he loved about her. He loved her. There, he'd said it, if only in his head.

Now he had to get them both out of there so he could say it aloud.

He pretended to consider the deal, though he was pretty sure the other man knew it was an act. Finally, he said, "What sort of assurance do I have that you'll actually keep your word and let us go?"

"None whatsoever. It's not like you'd believe me if I gave my word, so why should I bother?" Tiberius lifted a shoulder. "Let's put it this way—once I have the password, I'm out of here. I won't be back to this island— hell, I'm thinking of being done with the States for a while. Things are getting far too complicated with you around."

"Which is a perfect reason to kill me. Isn't that your usual MO?"

"I don't like being predictable." But something shifted in his eyes—game or not? Was the bastard lying, or did he want John to think he was? Glancing at his watch, Tiberius said, "I'm going to put you in with her now. You've got five minutes to get me that password, or the deal's off the table."

John barely heard the end of his response, though. His brain was locked on his first few words.

I don't like being predictable. It was what Grace had said, time and again, while working the computer banks in the Hoover building or over at Quantico. It had been a joke, because she'd been solid and dependable, and rarely broke pattern without checking with him first.

Or so it had seemed.

The moment the suspicion took root, it made far too much sense. He'd been too ready to blame the safe house attack on Sydney. Then, when the others had convinced him the bogus e-mail could've come from anywhere, he'd instinctively looked outside the team for suspects.

Now he realized it could just as easily have been Grace giving Tiberius the location, Grace giving him the positions of the other agents. She would've thought herself safe, not realizing that for whatever reason, Tiberius had decided she was expendable, that she'd be more use to him dead than alive, another layer of the game.

John felt a punch of guilt, both that he'd blamed her death on Sydney, and that Grace hadn't trusted him enough to tell him she was in trouble. In making himself safe from emotion, he'd made himself so unapproachable that he'd even driven away the members of his own team.

Well, that stopped now. He was stepping up as a leader and as a man. As soon as he figured out precisely how.

"Get going." One of the guards jabbed John with the butt of his rifle, prodding him toward the door. Two others closed around him, weapons drawn, and the three marched him out of the room while Tiberius remained in the security hub, no doubt planning to watch and listen in on everything that John and Sydney said to one another.

Fine, John thought. *Go ahead and listen. It's not going to be what you expect.*

The guards descended the marble stairs, boots ringing on stone, and escorted John down a long hallway with doors on either side. He tracked their progress against the blueprint inside his head and realized they were headed toward Sydney's old quarters, which were right near the lab space.

Something loosened inside him at the realization that she'd been stashed in relative safety, at least for the moment. But that left him not knowing where Michael, Drew and Jimmy were being kept, which could become a problem if they got free and needed to move fast.

Because he sure as hell didn't believe Tiberius. The

moment the bastard got the password, they were all as good as dead.

"In here." One of the guards swiped a key card and a door swung open. The other two covered John with their weapons, making the threat clear: *one wrong move and you're a wet spot on the floor.*

But they didn't need to worry, he didn't intend to try anything. Not yet, anyway.

Still, his gut was tight as he let the guards hustle him through the door, and the panel shut behind him.

Sydney stood in the center of the room, cheeks stained with tears. She looked at him, eyes filled with a mixture of wariness and hope, as though afraid to trust him to believe, when he'd been so ready to turn on her before.

He didn't say anything, simply crossed to her, opened his arms and gathered her close. He held her tight, feeling her heart beat in time with his. Dropping his cheek to her hair, he whispered, "I'm sorry about before, in the woods. I should've acted different. I wasn't mad, I swear. I didn't think you'd led them to us, I was just—" He broke off, not even sure he could explain it to himself.

On one level he'd been overjoyed to see her, on another, so terrified for her that he'd wanted to shake her, to hug her, to touch her all over until he was sure she was okay.

All of those feelings had sort of logjammed together in his brain and he'd wound up doing nothing.

"It's okay." Her arms snuck around his waist. "You were in agent mode. I get that." She drew in a shaky breath. "I didn't get it at the time, but I get it now."

"You're sure?" He eased away so he could look into her tearstained face. "You're okay?"

"Yeah." She used her hands to swipe at her cheeks. "You?"

"I'm scared."

"Excuse me?" The look on her face might've been comical under any other circumstance.

As it was, he drew her close again, feeling their time running out as he tried to find the words, tried to let her know that he got it now, he finally understood his own heart. "I'm scared that I'm going to mess this up, that I'm going to hurt you." He paused. "But I'm more scared by the thought of losing you. I don't want that. I want us to be together. I want to learn how to be the man you need, because whether either of us likes it or not, you're the woman I need. The woman I want."

When he paused, she said softly, "Say it."

He took a deep breath. "You're the woman I love." When his heart didn't stop beating at the words, when the world kept going on around them and time kept passing, he let out a long breath. "I love you. Please tell me I'm not too late."

SYDNEY WANTED to believe him. The need pounded in her bloodstream and spun through her soul, but she held herself back. What if this was another move in the game he'd been playing all along? What if—

That was just it, she realized. There were too many what-ifs. She could think of far too many reasons for him to say he loved her, and almost all of them seemed more plausible than believing he'd really, truly come around.

It was far more likely that he'd found another angle to play than believing he was ready to change.

"I'm sorry," she said softly, her heart breaking with the words. "I don't know how to believe you."

He closed his eyes on a wince of exquisite pain, then nodded sharply. "I understand. I can wait until you figure it out, because I'm not going anywhere this time. I promise."

Then, instead of turning away, he held her close. For a second, Sydney closed her eyes and simply absorbed the feel of him against her, and the sense of security—albeit false—that he brought her. Unable to do otherwise, she slid her hands up across his strong back and returned the embrace, pressing her cheek against his chest and letting his shirt absorb the moisture from her tears.

He brushed his lips across her temple, his lips barely moving as he whispered. "In about ninety seconds the guards are going to come back. I'm supposed to be convincing you to give up the password. He says if you do, he'll let all of us go."

Sydney stiffened. "Is that what this was all about? More games?"

He muttered a curse. "No. I was—and am—telling you the God's honest truth. About my feelings and about what's going to happen next. We don't have much time, so listen carefully. I want you to give him the password."

She started to pull away in shock, but he held her tightly, forestalling the move. That forced her to turn her face into his, so they were pressed cheek-to-cheek in a lover's embrace when she whispered, "Why?"

"Bringing Tiberius down is my responsibility, not yours. You more than did your duty by giving us all the information you did. Everything else was just…me being a blind, judgmental idiot, I guess."

A few days ago, even a few hours ago, she would've given anything to have him acknowledge such a thing.

Now it just ticked her off.

"No." She put her hands flat on his chest and pushed, creating enough distance that she could look up and glare at him. "You don't get to decide that now. You're at least partially responsible for me being back here, so you're darn well going to let me help fix what I did wrong." She leaned in and touched her lips to his in the briefest hint of a kiss, and felt the surprise vibrate through his big frame. But it was just another move in the game he'd drawn her into, because she used the kiss to murmur, "Now listen up. I have an idea, but you're going to have to trust me…."

Chapter Twelve

When she'd finished explaining the plan, John growled, "No. Just give him the password and let me take care of the rest."

"Sorry," she said stubbornly. "I don't take orders from you unless they make sense. These don't. Besides, my way will work. You just have to trust me."

And there it was.

"Is that what this is about?" he whispered. "Some sort of a test? It's not enough for me to tell you I believe you?"

That made her eyes go sad. She drew away and touched his face, skimming the back of her knuckles along his stubble-roughened jaw. "Poor John. So used to being suspicious you don't know how not to be."

And then their time was up. The door slid open behind them and the guards reentered, followed by Tiberius himself.

The scholarly-looking bastard saw John and Sydney wrapped together in an embrace and his lips twitched. "Touching. Just behave yourselves and you might live long enough to do it again."

When he moved toward them, John put himself in front of Sydney.

"Don't be stupidly heroic," Tiberius advised him. "You're outnumbered and outgunned." He paused. "Come on. Computer time." He gestured Sydney to the computer terminal sitting on a desk nearby, no doubt the one she'd used to work on her sequence late at night when she'd been unable to sleep.

John could picture her there, all alone, and his anger at Tiberius only increased.

"Not here," Sydney contradicted. "It's got to be done on the computer where the program was originally input, or it won't work."

Tiberius stared at her, unblinking. "I think you're bluffing."

"Are you willing to take that chance?"

He was silent so long John thought he wasn't going to agree. Then he did, turning away and jerking his head at the three guards. "Bring them to the lab. If either of them tries something, shoot them both. Leave the woman alive. If the agent dies, I won't be too upset."

The absolute unconcern in his voice was beyond chilling, giving a glimpse into the monster that lived within the professorial shell.

One of the guards grabbed Sydney and dragged her out into the hallway. John growled and lunged after the bastard, but the guard behind him slammed his rifle butt into John's kidneys, driving him to his knees.

"Enough," the guard behind him snapped. "Be glad there aren't any holes in your girlfriend. Yet."

The guards marched John and Sydney down the re-

mainder of the hallway to where it dead-ended in a set
of airlock-type doors that were plastered with biohaz-
ard decals and warnings. As they passed, John noticed
that several of the doors were ajar, where they'd been
closed and locked before. He caught a glimpse of living
quarters, bare, with a scattering of debris that looked like
a hasty evac.

He became aware of a low vibration running through
the floor beneath his feet and the air around them. At
first he thought it might be a generator running in the
basement, powering the big compound. But the noise
was new. He hadn't heard it before.

When they passed an exterior door that was locked
and barred, the sound became more distinct. It was a helicopter getting up to temp for takeoff. Beneath the
rotor-thump, he thought he heard the sound of boats
motoring off into the distance, as well.

Not a generator. A full-scale evacuation.

Time was running out.

One of the guards used his passkey to open the lab
doors, and John realized that was an indication that the
majority of the guards in the security hub were already
gone, because otherwise they would've been buzzed
in remotely.

As they moved through the doors into the lab, he caught
Sydney's eyes and saw the knowledge there. She nodded,
and he saw fear, but no sign that she was ready to give up.

I love you, he wanted to say again. He saw her eyes
widen fractionally, as though she'd read the sentiment in
his expression. Even thinking the words made him feel
bigger and meaner and ready to fight to protect his woman.

Before, he'd thought of love as something that would make him weaker. Instead, it was making him strong.

He could only hope it would make him tough enough to get Sydney and his team off the island before it blew.

"You said you needed the input terminal." Tiberius gestured to a row of low desks, each holding a computer connected to one or more pieces of high-tech lab equipment. "Do your thing." He glanced at his watch. "You've got ten minutes."

"Or?" she countered.

"Or I'll have my men shoot Agent Sharpe here, and you wouldn't want that, would you?"

Responding to his boss's threat, the guy behind John reversed his rifle, so it wasn't the butt poking into his kidneys anymore, but rather the business end of the weapon. Which complicated things, but only a little.

Sydney looked over at him one last time.

"Give him what he wants," John said. "He's won." He didn't have to fake the frustration in his voice. They were too close to checkmate for his comfort. Far too close.

Eyes filming, Sydney nodded and crossed to one of the terminals. Sitting at the roll-away desk chair, she tapped the mouse to wake the screen out of saver mode. The cursor blinked against a blank field, with a one-word question glowing on the screen: *Password?*

Sydney typed in something and hit Enter. The screen blanked for a second, then the same word returned: *Password?*

She typed in a second string and hit Enter, and again the screen blanked before the password prompt returned. She typed in a third string.

Before she could hit Enter, Tiberius warned in a low growl, "Don't play games with me, Sydney. You won't like what happens."

"I know what happens," she said softly, almost whispering. "I remember what you did to Jenny Marie."

Tiberius grabbed one of the guards' weapons and crossed to her. He pressed the gun barrel to her temple and leaned over her. "Then what are you doing?"

John held himself still, barely breathing, fighting the mad impulse to leap across the room and rip the bastard away from Sydney. Things only got worse when she turned a little and glanced at him, and he saw her lips frame the words, "I'm sorry."

Then she hit Enter.

The computer emitted a startled-sounding beep and the screen went dark. Half a second later, the power cut out completely, plunging them into darkness.

THE MOMENT THE LIGHTS went out, Sydney flung herself backward in the chair. It rolled a few feet before it hit something and overbalanced, spilling her to the floor. She hit hard and saw stars but kept rolling, desperate to get away from Tiberius.

Gunfire exploded in the close confines of the lab, and she could hear equipment smashing to pieces. The scientist in her cringed as her auto-sequencers and PCR machines bit the dust, but the emerging patriot in her—along with her human survival instincts—wanted only to get out of the lab.

She heard a crash nearby, a volley of gunshots and rapid-fire masculine cursing.

Then silence. A single set of running footsteps. The sound of a door opening and slamming shut. More silence.

The darkness pressed around Sydney, making her feel very small and alone all of a sudden. She huddled up against the flat plane of a wall, barely daring to breathe. Where was John? Was he dead? Captured?

Had he, God forbid, left her there alone, still playing his game?

No, she told herself firmly. *He wouldn't. He loves me. He said so and I believe him.*

Then, out of the darkness, his voice said, "Syd? You okay?"

Her breath exploded from her in a whoosh of relief. "I'm fine. You?"

"What did you do?"

"The first word killed the lab network permanently. The second and third together triggered another program that took the electric grid offline and FUBARed the rest of the networks on the island."

"Of course it did." But there was warmth in his voice rather than frustration. She heard the click of weaponry and clothing, presumably as he disarmed the guards he'd taken out. "Tiberius got away," he said after a moment.

Which explained the footsteps and slamming door, damn it. "Think we can catch him?"

There was a pause, and she could almost feel the internal battle before he said, "Let's find the others and get back to the boat. We'll get him another time."

"Which puts you back at square one," Sydney said. Guilt stabbed at her. "You're going to be back to hunting him without any really good connection to a prose-cutable crime. I'm sorry."

"I'm not." She heard him move closer, felt his arms come around her. "And I'm not exactly back where I started, either."

Then he kissed her, leaving no doubt as to his meaning.

She leaned into him as warmth speared through her. The darkness created warm intimacy even as the feel of a pistol in one of his hands, pressing into her back when he gathered her close against the hard wall of his chest, kept the sense of danger close by, adding to the thrill.

Heat bloomed as he slanted his mouth across hers and took it deeper, need spiraling up to become lust, desire becoming almost an obsession.

Yet alongside the physical sensations, new, scary emotions took root.

She was safe in his arms, yet exposed. She felt raw, her emotions too close to the surface, too uncertain. She'd thought she loved him, but what did she know about loving a man? He'd been a challenge, a conquest. There didn't seem to be any possible way for them to make it work. They were too different, and too alike in the wrong ways.

They were both stubborn and headstrong, and too used to running the show. If they tried to have a future, they'd probably wind up killing each other.

Then again, if they didn't get their butts in gear, their future—shared or separate—was down to twelve minutes or so.

They broke apart by unspoken accord. "Time to go," he said, voice rough with passion. He cleared his throat. "Here. Take this."

He pressed a weapon into her hand.

The small pistol was heavier than she would've imagined, and warm from his body heat. Her fingers curled around the grip and found the trigger. "Just point and shoot?"

"There's a safety." He guided her finger to the little sliding bump along one side of the trigger guard.

"Which one's off?"

"It's already off. Just leave it there for now…and yeah, with the safety off, it's point and shoot, but stick with me and it won't come to that, okay?"

"Promise?"

"I'll promise you whatever you want," he said simply.

The sentiment had her heart lodging in her throat as she began to believe he really meant it. He loved her. The very idea of it had worlds opening up before her even as the time ran out around them.

"What's the plan?" she asked, suddenly filled with renewed determination to get the hell off Rocky Cliff Island.

She'd done it once. She could do it again.

"Where do you think Tiberius is holding the others?"

She thought for a moment. "There are some wings I was never given access to." Those had been the blanks on the blueprints that they'd tried to fill in from satellite images and guesswork. "If I had to guess, I'd say he keeps his prisoners somewhere on the ground floor, north wing." She swallowed hard. "That's closest to the cliffs."

"Simplifying disposal of the bodies," he said, following her train of thought. "Right. Let's go."

He led her through the blackness. She only stumbled

once when her toe snagged on the cloth-covered, yielding surface of what she could only assume was one of the guards. She didn't ask if they were alive or dead. She wasn't sure she wanted to know.

When they reached the lab door, John cracked the panel and peeked into the hallway, which was slightly lighter than the lab, illuminated by daylight refracting from the living quarters through the half-open doors.

"Looks clear," he murmured, and led her out into the hallway.

They worked their way back up to the main entrance, then took the door to the north wing. After the third time John paused to check around a corner, Sydney whispered, "It seems like everyone's gone."

"The helicopter noise hasn't changed," he whispered. "That means Tiberius is still on the island."

"And I'm betting he's furious." For a second, she flashed back on Jenny Marie's screams and suppressed a shudder. She'd come way too far to back out now. Either they found a way to locate Tiberius and take him out, or she'd be spending the rest of her life in witness protection, with or without John.

She instinctively tightened her fingers on the gun he'd given her. The feel of the bulky grip was simultaneously reassuring and intimidating. She liked knowing she could protect herself, but couldn't picture herself shooting anyone.

Then again, if Tiberius was in her sights, she might be able to deal with it.

They checked the rooms one by one as they moved up the hallway. When they reached the sixth door, the one closest to the exit, they found it locked with a manual bolt in addition to the automatic locks, which had disengaged when the power cut out.

"Stand back," John warned. When Sydney was out of range, he fired twice, then kicked the door in. He went first, then beckoned her into what was clearly a holding area—and probably served a more grisly role, as well, given the overhead sprinkler system and prominent drain in the center of the waterproofed floor.

Michael, Jimmy and Drew sat against the far wall with their legs stretched out in front of them, bound at their ankles and their arms fastened behind their backs. They sent up a quiet cheer when they recognized the figures in the doorway.

"Sydney, here." John tossed her a knife, which he must've lifted from one of the guards back in the lab.

She fumbled the catch, trying not to drop the gun in her increasingly sweaty hands. Making an executive decision, she set the safety to 'on' and tucked the gun in her waistband, hoping like heck she'd gotten the on-off thing right.

Crouching down, she went to work on the bound men while John watched the doorway.

She freed Michael first and handed him the gun. "Here. You'll have more use for this than me."

"Thanks." He took the weapon and climbed to his feet, shaking out his stiff limbs as he went. Before he joined John at the door, though, he touched Sydney's shoulder briefly. "And thanks for guarding his back."

She grimaced. "I think I've gotten him into way more trouble than I've gotten him out of."

"You know what I mean."

Before she could respond, the sharpshooter moved off to join his leader. The two had a brief, low-voiced conversation while Sydney cut the zip ties binding the rest of the men.

When they were all up and the group was assembled near the door, John said, "We've got just about eight minutes on the countdown, so we're going to split up. I want Drew and Jimmy to head straight for the boat and have her ready to go. Michael and I are going out the front and straight down to the water. We'll meet you at the ropes."

Michael said, "Obviously grab weapons if you can, but don't waste time. And keep as low as you can—the chopper still hasn't lifted off. Best guess is that the bastard is waiting for us in the helo, and is going to open fire once we get near the boat. He's not going to want to let us get off the island. If we make it off, he'll target the boat."

"Any questions?" John asked.

"Just one." Sydney looked at him sideways. "Which group am I supposed to go with?"

"You're with me," John said, and there was a wealth of meaning in the words.

She smiled faintly. "Thanks."

"Don't thank me yet. We still have to get out of here." But he reached over and took her hand, right in front of everyone, and held on as though he needed the reassurance of the touch as much as she did. "Any other questions?"

When there weren't any, the team split and moved out, with the men promising to meet up at the ropes in under five minutes. That'd be cutting it close, but it was the best they were going to be able to do.

John led, with Sydney right behind him, and Michael bringing up the rear guard. They moved quickly through the mansion, eschewing stealth for speed. There were no more boat noises, only the thump of the idling helicopter.

"Do you think they cut your boat loose?" Sydney asked as they reached the front foyer, which seemed even colder and more impersonal with the sense of emptiness that echoed throughout the mansion, and the lack of the normal blowers and low-grade beeps coming from electrical systems that'd gone dead thanks to the worm program.

"Unless you have a better suggestion, we're going to assume it's still there," John responded with a hint of an edge in his voice.

"Sorry," she said. "You're right. Don't ask unless it's something we can fix."

He blew out a breath and squeezed her hand, which he was still holding. "I didn't mean to snap. I just wish I had a better answer."

She squeezed back. "I think we're just about due for a lucky break, don't you?"

"If you say so." But he smiled and touched his lips to hers. Then he pulled away, readied his weapon and went into agent mode. "Ready?" he asked Michael.

The sharpshooter nodded. "Let's move out."

They were halfway across the cleared lawn area surrounding the mansion when the first shot rang out, coming from the direction of one of the guard shacks. John immediately spun Sydney and shoved her toward a stand of trees nearby. "Get under cover. I'm right behind you."

Heart pounding in her chest, she didn't stop to argue or ask questions. She bolted for safety, crashing through the thick brush while the men opened fire behind her, retreating along the path they'd come up only an hour or so earlier.

Sydney took two steps past the trees, stumbled and went down. The impact knocked her breath away, and she lay dazed for a second, the sound of gunfire muted by the ringing in her ears. It took her a moment to focus. When she did, she saw the tripwire that'd taken her down.

Then she saw a pair of loafers appear, topped by cabled pants and a tweed jacket, with Tiberius's face looming far above.

His mouth split in a wide, patronizing smile.

And everything went black.

Chapter Thirteen

The attack stopped abruptly. One minute they were taking heavy fire from three positions on the mansion side of the clearing, and the next there was a silence so complete it put John's instincts into overdrive.

That hadn't been an attack, he realized. It'd been a distraction.

He spun and bolted for the trees. "Sydney!"

There was no answer, and when he reached the clearing there was no Sydney. She was gone.

A week ago, even a day ago, his first thought would've been that she'd betrayed him, but not now. He knew her better than that, trusted her more than that, and he didn't even break stride before reversing course and returning to Michael. "Tiberius has her," he reported tersely. "They'll be headed for the helicopter."

The sharpshooter didn't hesitate. "Then that's where we're going."

They headed for higher ground, and the sound of the helicopter rotor-thump. The detour was going to take time they didn't have to spare, but there was no discussion as they melted into the trees and headed for the helipad. Sydney was one of them now, and they weren't leaving her behind.

SYDNEY'S HEAD was buzzing when she regained consciousness. Or rather, there was a buzzing noise all around her, she realized as her surroundings started to come clear.

She was lying on her side against a wall of cargo netting, which held stacked boxes and trunks in place. The hard surface beneath her vibrated at an increasing frequency as the pitch of the hum increased. The whole world seemed to shudder, then sway, and the hum became the roar of an engine.

She was on the helicopter!

Panic slashed through her. She exploded into motion, only to find herself brought up short by bindings at her wrists and ankles. They gave slightly, but cut into her skin. Zip ties. And they were attached to the cargo netting, leaving her trapped, lying helpless on her side at the rear of the large, twin-rotor helicopter's cargo bay.

She was facing the forward passenger compartment and the cockpit beyond, and the light from a rolled-open side slider showed four men ahead of her: the pilot and copilot, both wearing guard uniforms, one other guard and Tiberius.

She must've made some sound while waking up, because Tiberius turned around in his seat to look at her.

He shook his head as though she'd deeply disappointed him. "Blanking the computer banks was a bad move, Sydney. And here I thought you were one of the smart ones. Turns out you're just as stupid—and idealistic—as your boyfriend." When the engine note changed again, he glanced at the pilot. "We good to go yet?"

"Almost, sir. The chips controlling the pressure gauges are just about done rebooting. I'm just lucky I logged out of the network when I did, or her program would've taken out the entire system."

Tiberius glanced at his watch. "You have five minutes to get us over the water."

The chopper dipped and spun unsteadily, and the motion slid Sydney a few more inches along the deck until she came to a stop at the farthest reaches of her bonds. Her new position gave her a glimpse out the side door, enough to let her know they were still on the island.

More importantly, she caught a flash of motion from the treeline. John.

"What are you going to do to me?" she said sharply, trying to draw Tiberius's attention.

He turned back to her and raised an eyebrow. "Well, I'm certainly not stupid. I'm going to chuck you once we're over open water."

His flat-affect delivery was equally as terrifying as the threat itself, and Sydney didn't have to fake the tremor in her voice when she said, "I can re-create the virus. I know the shortcuts now. I can do it in half the time it took me before."

"I'm through making deals with you," he said, flicking his fingers in dismissal. "You can't be trusted to stay bought. Not a very admirable quality."

She dropped her voice. "Try me. I'll make it worth your while." She paused, and when he didn't turn away immediately, said, "The technology's not just limited to DNA testing, you know. I bet I could program the vector to recognize a specific DNA fingerprint and kill just that one person. You wouldn't need to be anywhere near the target. Just leave some of the virus where he'll come into contact with it. Poof. Murder by long distance."

She had his full attention now. "You're saying you could make such a thing?"

"Imagine the possibilities," she said, trying to make him believe she'd throw herself fully on his side, if only to ensure her life. "If the target has DNA on file in one of the databases, you wouldn't even need a DNA sample. You could just lift the repeat numbers from the database, and poof. They're dead."

Frowning, he said, "It wouldn't work if the target has been infected with the other bug, right? The fingerprint would be too blurry for the virus to lock on to."

Triumph spurted. She had him considering it now. "I won't know for sure until I've tested the actual constructs, but even if that's the case, what's the downside? If someone wanted to block themselves from the fingerprint-targeting vector, they'd have to buy the fingerprint-blurring vector from you. Either way you're getting paid. It's a win-win."

She was making herself sick even thinking this way, let alone saying it aloud. Worse, John could hear her. What was he thinking as he listened in?

Tiberius's eyes flashed. "If this stuff is so easy to conceptualize, why do I need you? I should be able to give the theory to another scientist—one who'll stay bought—and have him turn it around with far less risk."

She met his eyes and willed him to see nothing but what she wanted him to when she said, "Are you willing to take that gamble?"

Before he could answer, the engine note changed to a deeper, full-throated growl, the helicopter stabilized and the pilot called, "All set, sir!"

Tiberius turned. "Then get us out of here." He was turning back to Sydney when his attention fixed on something outside the open slider. He shouted and grabbed for the guard sitting beside him.

And all hell broke loose.

John lunged onto the helicopter, followed by Michael. Just then, the craft lifted off the ground, wallowing with the added weight. The guard beside Tiberius leapt from his chair and opened fire, causing the pilot and copilot to duck and swear. The chopper dipped and swayed, bouncing off the ground and rattling the men locked in hand-to-hand combat in the passenger cabin.

John grappled with Tiberius, whose face was etched with rage. John, on the other hand, maintained his icy calm as he struggled to subdue the other man, while looking around the small cabin.

The ice cracked when he saw Sydney.

"Take him!" He shoved Tiberius at Michael, who caught the older man with a good punch along the jaw.

Then John was kneeling beside her, cutting the zip ties away and helping her up, and the only thing in his eyes was concern and love. For her.

"I didn't mean any of those things I said to him." She

gripped his wrists, willing him to believe her. "I never would've built such a thing."

"I know. Don't worry about it." He touched his lips to hers. "I'll have to admit that your brain is a pretty scary place, though."

She grinned and started to laugh, but the laughter was cut off by a bark of gunfire and a sudden flurry of activity from up ahead as Michael flew backward out of the helicopter. The guard was down and unmoving, but the chopper was gaining altitude as the load lightened.

"John!" Sydney cried, her heart lunging into her throat at the realization that they were seconds away from being trapped on Tiberius's helicopter, heading out over open water.

"Stay back," he ordered, "and get out the door as soon as you can. I'll be right behind you."

Before she could answer, he'd rushed Tiberius. His momentum drove them away from the door and he shouted, "Sydney, go!"

She dove through headfirst, not realizing that the craft was a good ten feet off the ground and rising fast. Screaming, she grabbed on to one of the skids and held on for dear life, her feet dangling in thin air. "John, *help!*"

There were three shots in quick succession, coming from inside the helicopter, but she couldn't tell who was shooting or who'd been shot.

"Sydney, let go," Michael yelled from below. "I'll catch you!"

She didn't think or argue. She closed her eyes and let go.

Her stomach jumped into her throat in a moment of free fall, and then she hit, taking Michael down in a tangle of arms and legs.

Above them, the helicopter took flight, banking and soaring away with one member of the team still on board.

"John!" Sydney surged to her feet and reached for the aircraft, though that was futile. *"John!"*

"Sydney!" Michael dragged her back. "Come on, we've got to go."

The urgency in his voice pierced the terror and anguish of seeing the chopper grow smaller, and she remembered the countdown.

How much time was left?

Seeing he had her attention, Michael started jogging downhill, toward the cliffs. "Come on!"

They fled toward the cliffs where the boat should be, reaching the ropes in under three minutes. Sydney stumbled to a halt at the sight of a man waiting for them, but it was Jimmy. One of the good guys. "Hurry!" he shouted. "Move!"

They moved. The cliff descent was a blur of gravity and burning palms to Sydney, and she hit the beach running. Drew grabbed her and boosted her up and over the edge of the boat, and the others followed moments later. Then they were casting off, and Michael was gunning the boat away from the island.

"Use the riptide," Drew shouted over the crash of waves and the laboring noise of the boat's engine.

"Doesn't matter where we go, just so long as it's away from the island!"

Michael nodded and sent the skiff toward a section of flatter-looking water that was all moving in one direction, forming what looked like a river within the ocean swells. When they hit the current, the skiff leapt forward, forcing them to hang on for the ride.

Sydney hung on, but she couldn't make herself do any more than that. Her entire attention was fixed on the empty sky, while Tiberius's words rang in her ears: *I'm certainly not stupid,* he'd said. *I'm going to chuck you once we're over open water.*

Only he'd be tossing John's body, not hers.

Tears filled her eyes and grief hollowed her out until she was nothing but a shell of sadness, nothing but regret. In the end, he'd trusted her. He'd known she was lying to Tiberius about the virus, and hadn't doubted her for an instant. She should've told him she loved him right then, when she'd had the chance.

Now it was too late.

"Don't give up on him yet," Michael said, coming up beside her and dropping a blanket over her shoulders. "Sharpe is the Iceman. If anyone can gain control of the chopper and bring Tiberius in, it'll be him."

"He would've won if he hadn't been worried about rescuing me," she said softly, staring at her fingers twined in her lap. "I messed him up, made him weaker."

"Not necessarily. You gave him something to come back to." Now Michael was looking up at the stubbornly empty sky, too, as were Jimmy and Drew, but to no avail.

Then Jimmy pointed. "There! Do you see it?"

Sydney lunged to her feet and grabbed the gunwale. "Where?"

Seconds later, the island exploded behind them with the sound of a thousand subway trains crashing into each other at once.

Sydney screamed as the shockwave slammed into the boat, rolling it up on one side and leaving it poised there for a second before it hurtled back down into a trough, shuddering with the impact. Heat scorched the exposed skin of her hands and face, and shrapnel peppered down around them, large and small pieces of island debris, chunks of masonry and wood stinging her where they hit.

It took her a second to realize she was alone at the railing. "Michael!" she screamed, looking around, to where the others were picking themselves up off the deck, checking small injuries and shrapnel hits. "Where's Michael?"

Seconds later, Drew went over the side and struck out swimming toward Michael's motionless body, which was floating facedown in the water.

Drew was in the process of hauling Michael back to the boat, swimming one-handed, when a new sound became audible over the fading rumble of the explosion.

Helicopter rotors.

Heart lunging into her throat, Sydney searched the sky but saw nothing more than she'd seen before, save for the section of sky obscured by a thick pillar of smoke and debris pouring from the wreckage that had been Tiberius's island.

Then the noise increased and the chopper appeared from behind the smoky curtain, creating mad swirls of soot in the air.

John! she wanted to scream, but couldn't because her throat was locked on the word, on the very act of breathing as the helicopter drew near.

"Grab him!" Jimmy shouted behind her. There was a flurry of motion, and the boat tipped slightly as Jimmy and Drew struggled to get Michael on board.

"He's breathing," Drew reported, at the same moment Jimmy shouted, "Get us the hell out of here. Chopper incoming!"

Sure enough, the aircraft swept in a slow arc and headed straight for the boat.

For a split second the future hovered between salvation and destruction. Then the men on the chopper opened fire.

"Down!" Drew shouted, though they were already scrambling for the scant cover available on the sturdy boat.

With Michael down, Drew took over the controls and sent the skiff hurtling in a series of evasive maneuvers, slewing the craft wildly from side to side and avoiding the first strafing run as the chopper passed overhead. The pilot corrected quickly, though, and lined up for another run.

"There's the *Valiant!*" Jimmy cried, pointing to a dot on the horizon.

The skiff hurtled in the direction of the coast guard ship with the helicopter right behind it, but the men on the chopper didn't fire again. Instead, the aircraft began to wallow from side to side, as though it was having mechanical difficulties.

Or someone on board was putting up a hell of a fight.

"Almost in range of the *Valiant*'s launcher," Drew called, still swerving the boat in a series of evasive runs. "One minute."

It took a moment for that to penetrate. When it did, Sydney spun to the others. "They're not going to shoot the chopper, are they? They can't! They—"

She broke off when the door in the side of the helicopter slid open and a body pitched out and fell limply for twenty feet or so to the sea. Sydney screamed, and screamed again when the helicopter suddenly swerved in the sky, seeming to be coming for them again.

"Fire, damn it!" Drew shouted, though the approaching coast guard cutter was too far away for anyone to hear, and the rotor-thump drowned out the shout as the helicopter approached.

Then without warning, it swerved hard to the left, flipped up and over and began to autorotate, spinning like a flat disk as it hurtled back toward the island. The engines screamed and smoke began to pour from the open door.

Seconds later, it slammed into the cliff below the wrecked mansion, detonated in an orange-red fireball and crashed into the ocean.

Seconds after that, it was gone, marked only by a sooty smudge on the rocky cliff face.

Someone was moaning. It took Sydney a minute to realize it was her, and to feel the bite of pain where she'd dug her fingertips into the metal side of the boat, and broken two of her fingernails away. "No," she said, "no, no, no."

But the litany of denial didn't bring the helicopter back up to the surface, and it didn't make John suddenly appear, treading water and waving for a pickup.

The sea was eerily calm.

"He jumped," Michael said, his voice ragged. He was bleeding from a cut on his head, but he was conscious and standing. "That had to be him. He got out before they hit."

Drew sent the boat toward where the jumper had landed. The *Valiant* approached the same point from the other side, and all hands were on deck, scanning the water for a swimmer.

Or a body, Sydney thought as a big shiver crawled down her spine and made her stomach pitch. *Please be there,* she thought desperately. *Please be okay.* The chant repeated itself over and over again in her head, but she saw nothing. No swimmer. No body. Just water.

Tears blinded her and broke free, tracking down her cheeks. Michael moved up beside her along the railing, Jimmy and Drew stepping to her other side, so the four of them stood together, scanning the Atlantic for the leader of their team. For the man she loved.

"Ahoy the boat."

For a second, Sydney didn't think she'd actually heard the hail, which had come from the other side of the boat, the side away from where the body had fallen.

Then she heard it again. "Hello? Anyone up there?"

It was John's voice.

Screaming his name, she flew to the other side of the

boat, with the others right behind her. And there he was, treading water.

His eyes locked on her and a huge smile split his face. "You're okay."

"Yeah," she said, grinning through her tears. "I am now."

He held up a hand. "A little help here?"

Michael, Jimmy and Drew were only too happy to drag him aboard the skiff, and the team surrounded him with backslaps and congratulations, but his attention stayed fixed on Sydney, and all of his emotions were plain to see.

There was satisfaction of a job well done in bringing Tiberius to justice, one way or another. There was relief that it was over and they were both standing safely on the deck.

And there was love, shining clear as the sunlight, along with the question she hadn't yet answered.

She answered it now as he crossed to her, opening her arms to him. "I love you."

He whooped and swept her up in an embrace that might have been cold and wet from the seawater that still poured from him, but was warm where it counted— where their lips touched, and where their bodies melded together in a long, satisfying kiss.

She wrapped her arms around him, so this time, unlike the first time they'd washed up on a deck together just off Rocky Cliff Island, they shared the same blanket.

Epilogue

The six months following Tiberius's death were harder work than John had expected. He and his team had been forced to go in and dismantle certain pieces of his organization by force, and they'd been fighting a constant rearguard action to keep others from stepping into the leadership role.

Eventually someone would step up, he knew. Nature abhorred a vacuum. But the prospect didn't bother him nearly as much as it had before, because he was coming to realize that was part of the game, too. It wasn't just the moves leading up to checkmate that mattered, it was what the victor did after the game.

Before, he would've headed home for a few weeks of vacation and lasted only a few days before restlessness sent him back to the office.

Now, as he turned into the long drive leading to his house and rolled past the freshly clipped paddocks, where a pair of fat quarter horses dozed in the sun, tails swishing idly at the last of the season's flies, he knew he'd be squeezing every last drop out of this vacation, because everything was different now.

These days, he had a reason to come home.

He found her in the kitchen, cooking an army's worth of pasta and sauce with her usual combination of a scientist's precision and risk-taker's flare. When he wrapped his arms around her slim waist and pressed his lips into the curve of her neck, she leaned back into him for a moment, then turned in his arms to greet him with a proper kiss, one that had him thinking of turning down the burners and nipping upstairs.

"Company will be here in thirty," she murmured against his lips as hers curved in a smile. "Hold that thought, okay?"

Knowing it would be better for the wait—and the time to explore the ever-changing, always-blinding heat between them—he kissed her nose and grinned. "We celebrating?"

He figured he already knew the answer from her smile.

"The accelerated approval came through today," she confirmed. "We've got the go-ahead to start Celeste on the new treatment." She reached past him to give the pasta a quick stir, which involved pressing her hips against his erection, wringing a groan from him.

"Congratulations." He nibbled at her ear. "Temptress."

Her eyes glazed and her breath started coming faster, in the little puffs of excitement he loved so much. "Thanks." She tipped her head back and moaned a little as he moved to her throat and along the soft line of her jaw. "There's no guarantee it'll work, but all the early results are good. At a minimum, we should be able to stop the disease from progressing further. At best, she could get some of the feeling and strength back in her arms." She turned her lips to his and drew him into a deep, searching kiss. When it ended, she whispered, "I couldn't have done it without you."

In the aftermath of the op on Rocky Cliff Island, he'd gone to bat for her, not just to keep her safe from prosecution, but to get her added on to a government-affiliated think tank investigating ways to make—and counteract—various types of bioweapons.

He smiled against her mouth, turning down the burner when the water boiled over. "I figured the U.S. of A. was far safer with you working *for* the government rather than against it." He'd also made it a condition that the think tank had to support her side project of developing a cure for Singer's syndrome.

Her bug wasn't perfect yet, but it was getting there.

When her fingers went to his belt, he glanced at the kitchen clock. "Thirty minutes, you said?"

"Mmm." She followed the direction of his gaze. "Twenty-five now, but it's Celeste and Hugo. They'll understand if dinner's not done. And besides, I'm sure they can amuse themselves…or each other." Her eyes glittered, no doubt at the thought of the relationship that had developed between her sister and the FBI agent who'd protected her during the dangers of earlier that year.

With that, she flicked off the burner beneath the boiling water and turned the sauce down to simmer.

Then, without a word, she held out a hand and they walked up the stairs together.

As they stepped into the bedroom, he leaned close and whispered, "I love you."

She looked up at him, eyes gleaming. "I hope you know you've said that once or twice before."

He smiled, swept her up in his arms and carried her to their bed. "Then I guess that means I finally found something worth repeating."

* * * * *

THOROUGHBRED LEGACY
The stakes are high when it comes to love,
horse racing, family secrets
and broken promises.

A new exciting Harlequin continuity series
coming soon!
Led by New York Times *bestselling author*
Elizabeth Bevarly
FLIRTING WITH TROUBLE

Here's a preview!

THE DOOR CLOSED behind them, throwing them into darkness and leaving them utterly alone. And the next thing Daniel knew, he heard himself saying, "Marnie, I'm sorry about the way things turned out in Del Mar."

She said nothing at first, only strode across the room and stared out the window beside him. Although he couldn't see her well in the darkness—he still hadn't switched on a light…but then, neither had she—he imagined her expression was a little preoccupied, a little anxious, a little confused.

Finally, very softly, she said, "Are you?"

He nodded, then, worried she wouldn't be able to see the gesture, added, "Yeah. I am. I should have said goodbye to you."

"Yes, you should have."

Actually, he thought, there were a lot of things he should have done in Del Mar. He'd had *a lot* riding on the Pacific Classic, and even more on his entry, Little Joe, but after meeting Marnie, the Pacific Classic had been the last thing on Daniel's mind. His loss at Del Mar had pretty much ended his career before it had even begun, and he'd had to start all over again, rebuilding from nothing.

He simply had not then and did not now have room
in his life for a woman as potent as Marnie Roberts. He
was a horseman first and foremost. From the time he
was a schoolboy, he'd known what he wanted to do
with his life—be the best possible trainer he could be.

He had to make sure Marnie understood—and he
understood, too—why things had ended the way they
had eight years ago. He just wished he could find the
words to do that. Hell, he wished he could find the
thoughts to do that.

"You made me forget things, Marnie, things that I
really needed to remember. And that scared the hell out
of me. Little Joe should have won the Classic. He was
by far the best horse entered in that race. But I didn't
give him the attention he needed and deserved that
week, because all I could think about was you. Hell,
when I woke up that morning all I wanted to do was lie
there and look at you, and then wake you up and make
love to you again. If I hadn't left when I did—the way
I did—I might still be lying there in that bed with you,
thinking about nothing else."

"And would that be so terrible?" she asked.

"Of course not," he told her. "But that wasn't why I
was in Del Mar," he repeated. "I was in Del Mar to win
a race. That was my job. And my work was the most important thing to me."

She said nothing for a moment, only studied his face
in the darkness as if looking for the answer to a very important question. Finally she asked, "And what's the
most important thing to you now, Daniel?"

Wasn't the answer to that obvious? "My work," he
answered automatically.

She nodded slowly. "Of course," she said softly. "That is, after all, what you do best."

Her comment, too, puzzled him. She made it sound as if being good at what he did was a bad thing.

She bit her lip thoughtfully, her eyes fixed on his, glimmering in the scant moonlight that was filtering through the window. And damned if Daniel didn't find himself wanting to pull her into his arms and kiss her. But as much as it might have felt as if no time had passed since Del Mar, there were eight years between now and then. And eight years was a long time in the best of circumstances. For Daniel and Marnie, it was virtually a lifetime.

So Daniel turned and started for the door, then halted. He couldn't just walk away and leave things as they were, unsettled. He'd done that eight years ago and regretted it.

"It *was* good to see you again, Marnie," he said softly. And since he was being honest, he added, "I hope we see each other again."

She didn't say anything in response, only stood silhouetted against the window with her arms wrapped around her in a way that made him wonder whether she was doing it because she was cold, or if she just needed something—someone—to hold on to. In either case, Daniel understood. There was an emptiness clinging to him that he suspected would be there for a long time.

* * * * *

THOROUGHBRED LEGACY
coming soon wherever books are sold!

Thoroughbred *Legacy*

Launching in June 2008

A dramatic new 12-book continuity that embodies the American Dream.

Meet the Prestons, owners of Quest Stables, a successful horse-racing and breeding empire. But the lives, loves and reputations of this hardworking family are put at risk when a breeding scandal unfolds.

Flirting with Trouble

by *New York Times* bestselling author

ELIZABETH BEVARLY

Eight years ago, publicist Marnie Roberts spent seven days of bliss with Australian horse trainer Daniel Whittleson. But just as quickly, he disappeared. Now Marnie is heading to Australia to finally confront the man she's never been able to forget.

The stakes are high when it comes to love, horse racing, family secrets and broken promises.

A new exciting Harlequin continuity series coming soon!

Silhouette®

Desire

Cole's Red-Hot Pursuit

Cole Westmoreland is a man who gets what he
wants. And he wants independent and sultry
Patrina Forman! She resists him—until a Montana
blizzard traps them together. For three delicious
nights, Cole indulges Patrina with his brand of
seduction. When the sun comes out, Cole and
Patrina are left to wonder—will this be the end of
the passion that storms between them?

Look for

COLE'S RED-HOT PURSUIT

by USA TODAY bestselling author

BRENDA JACKSON

Available in June 2008 wherever you buy books.

Always Powerful, Passionate and Provocative.

™ **Silhouette**®

Romantic
SUSPENSE

Sparked by Danger,
Fueled by Passion.

Seduction Summer:
Seduction in the sand…and a killer on the beach.

Silhouette Romantic Suspense invites you to the hottest
summer yet with three connected stories from some
of our steamiest storytellers! Get ready for…

Killer Temptation
by **Nina Bruhns;**
a millionaire this tempting is worth a little danger.

Killer Passion
by **Sheri WhiteFeather;**
an FBI profiler's forbidden passion incites a
killer's rage,

and

Killer Affair
by **Cindy Dees;**
this affair with a mystery man is to die for.

Look for

KILLER TEMPTATION by Nina Bruhns in June 2008
KILLER PASSION by Sheri WhiteFeather in July 2008
and
KILLER AFFAIR by Cindy Dees in August 2008.

Available wherever you buy books!

Visit Silhouette Books at www.eHarlequin.com   SRS27586

REQUEST YOUR FREE BOOKS!

2 FREE NOVELS
PLUS 2
FREE GIFTS!

◆ HARLEQUIN®

INTRIGUE®

Breathtaking Romantic Suspense

YES! Please send me 2 FREE Harlequin Intrigue® novels and my 2 FREE gifts (gifts are worth about $10). After receiving them, if I don't wish to receive any more books, I can return the shipping statement marked "cancel." If I don't cancel, I will receive 6 brand-new novels every month and be billed just $4.24 per book in the U.S. or $4.99 per book in Canada, plus 25¢ shipping and handling per book and applicable taxes, if any*. That's a savings of close to 15% off the cover price! I understand that accepting the 2 free books and gifts places me under no obligation to buy anything. I can always return a shipment and cancel at any time. Even if I never buy another book from Harlequin, the two free books and gifts are mine to keep forever.

182 HDN EEZ7   382 HDN EEZK

Name	(PLEASE PRINT)	

Address		Apt. #

City	State/Prov.	Zip/Postal Code

Signature (if under 18, a parent or guardian must sign)

Mail to the **Harlequin Reader Service:**
IN U.S.A.: P.O. Box 1867, Buffalo, NY 14240-1867
IN CANADA: P.O. Box 609, Fort Erie, Ontario L2A 5X3

Not valid to current subscribers of Harlequin Intrigue books.

Want to try two free books from another line?
Call 1-800-873-8635 or visit www.morefreebooks.com.

* Terms and prices subject to change without notice. N.Y. residents add applicable sales tax. Canadian residents will be charged applicable provincial taxes and GST. This offer is limited to one order per household. All orders subject to approval. Credit or debit balances in a customer's account(s) may be offset by any other outstanding balance owed by or to the customer. Please allow 4 to 6 weeks for delivery. Offer available while quantities last.

Your Privacy: Harlequin is committed to protecting your privacy. Our Privacy Policy is available online at www.eHarlequin.com or upon request from the Reader Service. From time to time we make our lists of customers available to reputable third parties who may have a product or service of interest to you. If you would prefer we not share your name and address, please check here. ☐

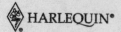